Dedicated to:

Doreen Tallack – Mum:
had it ready in time - sa

CU00662197

The real disco crowd:

Mario, Alison, Ron, Pip, Paul, Simon, Phil, Carol, Cindy, Andy.

Thanks for the lifts, the friendship, the music, the take-aways.

Juleka Nwankwo for help with the production and the first draft

The cast of *The Early Days of Disco* theatre production; first performed at The Hen and Chickens theatre in 2008. Thanks for making it happen:

James Hedges

Yasmine Maya

Richard Medhurst – Assistant Director

Richard Roberts

Christopher Tajah

Jodie Tranter

Leila Travis

Thanks to:

Stephen French and Rae Benjamin for the cover shoot –
Venice Beach.

List of Chapters:

Part One

1: Portsmouth:

New Year's Eve 1979.

The Tribal Rites of Granny's Night.

Taxi-drivers...

Super cool – the way they bring that quiet, white limousine to a halt, the way he looks with disappointment at the change you've managed to collect, so you decide to impress and tell him to 'keep it' - like a true Rockefeller - just like they do in the films even though you've only five quid left for the next four days. You place him up there with the exalted McDonalds' serving girl and those super-cool nightclub bar-staff - people who *know* the nightlife, they *know* the secrets, let's face it - they're where it's at. You casually throw the door shut of the quiet, sumptuous world of the cab and brace yourself for the reckoning ahead. It doesn't shut properly, so you try and push it to – now it's caught on the latch – 'hang on' you call to the driver as you re-open the door and then slam it – this time far too hard. You hear the muffled curse. He drives away. Move on.

'Nice' says Tony in his cream suit.

'Bollocks' you reply in your 'Tuf' lace ups from school.

You look up at the celebration of cement that is the Tricorn shopping centre; lost, empty and threatening like a Kraftwerk single at the midnight hour, shuffle into the lift and the battered doors unevenly shudder shut behind you; two floors up, the doors slide open and reveal, not a car-park but a velvet curtain, a muffled bass, two men in dickie bows and dinner jackets face you. You walk towards them...

The curtains part, somehow the dickie bows nod and the bass interrupts your thoughts as a girl in a cat suit walks past with drinks and all at once you hear the opening of Sylvester's 'Do Ya Wanna Funk' screaming through the glitter and the flashing shadows from the strobe as that short haired brunette in skin-tight neon blue sidles up and runs her back against you – yes you - before she smiles and disappears amidst the whirling deck shoes and soul boy hair-cuts; but then those glossy high heels flicker whilst the music beckons you in; there's gloss black, spinning purple and she's now five yards away - and her silver necklace glistens like mercury on porcelain and her smile is from that album cover and already you're in love and that must have been 'it'? *The* signal and this is going to be *the* night - the time to take action. So much potential... as you survey the field of battle as the instrumental kicks in and you're transported to the streets of New York – far away from Portsmouth - and the laughing, waving blonde girls and it's like you're in some Coke advert and you're not from the Hill Park estate and you don't work at the dole office and right now you *are* the guys from 5th Avenue. So here goes...

'Right, you ready?

'Ready for what?' As if you didn't know.

'Move in.'

'Now?'

'Why not?'

'Why not? Because she's out of my league – how about that for a reason? – Pernod!'

You shout in the direction of the bar and here you find safety as the striped waist-coated slicked-back hair dude takes your order with a nonchalant nod and you wish you were him – wondering which yacht or luxury flat he lives in because this is the high life - and there's the palatial podium of the DJ booth with flashes of vinyl catching the rotating purple lights and this is the nearest you'll get to Las Vegas.

'What you reckon?' You motion towards the floor where three dancing queens with big hair, headbands and heels twist their bodies like they rule the night.

'Nah'. Says Tony, already in tune with your eye-line.

Terry bounces up from nowhere, going for the Miami-Vice loose tie effect but all you can think of is the Shoestring detective series.

'Shall we, then?'

He knows it's rhetorical... nevertheless, undeterred, he motions towards the three lethal women who flash and reflect the lights from their heels and handbags, one shoulder bare, greens and burgundy and yellows – the colours of the decade - you have never even spoken to such dangerous human beings and have no idea how to even start but consider it a duty as an eighteen-year-old. You only have visual signs to communicate with as the Bose speakers overhead are kicking out a treble that is hitting your eardrums like needles. You nod to Terry (who's already started to dance) as if you heard and you agree and move purposely away from under the speakers, past the heels and over the handbags before arriving at the bar again. He's seen this before, so he shrugs, strides forward from the bar and casually walks over the cliff-edge of potential shame and actually asks a gold dress to dance – a real, proper actual woman - in a gold dress. She accepts. Unbelievable. No shame, no injuries, no emotional damage, no ridicule, no refusal, no broken leg, no bruises at all. A real live woman, in a gold dress, dancing with Terry.

Tony, quieter, shiny burgundy shirt, keeps you company at the refuge. You hope his coolness of dress code somehow rubs off on your own one-time school-wear of fluffy, worn green shirt and those lace-up school shoes. You both survey the floor and note the short-haired brunette girl in the electric neon blue dress and her long blonde haired floaty friend in something silver. The more you watch the further away they seem to get.

'Come on - what would John Travolta do?'

'Bide his time.'

'No, he wouldn't, he'd say – '

'He wouldn't say anything - he'd just give her a look.'

'Give her a look then.

'She can't see me.'

'Well get where she can.'

'Anyway, in the film they ask *him* to dance.'

'Yeah, in the film.'

'Exactly. So, I should wait.'

'Oh, I see - they're gonna come to you, are they?'

'Eventually.'

'Yeah well we've only got four hours' - and you feel
the three bass notes repeated before you hear them,
before you know it's Jackson and 'Don't Stop til' you
get enough' with Malcolm (Cortina estate) and Mark
motioning us all out and for a moment you're part of
the scene and everyone's dancing; the exotic,
dangerous high heels are just three feet away – they
might as well be Charlie's Angels and you might as
well be driving over the Brooklyn Bridge on your way
to Studio 54, such is the life you're leading right now;
because maybe a bit of nervousness is only normal
and maybe you're doing all right here after all, maybe
you're blending in quite nicely and finding your
confidence, maybe the shirt doesn't matter, or maybe
the lace up shoes aren't being noticed right now;

maybe you're dancing, even though you feel like a sack of shit, maybe feeling like an idiot doesn't always mean you look like an idiot… maybe…

The confidence grows, you're on the floor, the brass section kicks out and Jackson screams like he's in the room such are the speakers.

'Relax more' shouts Tony in your ear whilst dancing in his characteristic 'Bruce Lee' style of dancing without dancing, for there appears to be no effort in his dance, he just moves with the music, like he's actually enjoying it - and you have no idea how he does this.

'Ah… okay…' so, you do – you try very hard, very aggressively… to relax more. This doesn't feel right all of a sudden, kinda like it felt when you started dancing thirty seconds a go.

'Listen to the beat.'

So, you listen as hard as you can.

'And bend your knees'.

So you aggressively relax, listen to the music and bend the knees feeling more like a malfunctioning robot than ever before – which means by your current learning curve you probably look like one too, which is bad. So, you decide that you want to get off the floor now so you must somehow find safety, or make a bold move... and at such times you realise your inner soul is bared – but not the dancing, musical soul of Soul Train – no - you go over the top and start mimicking really bad dancing to hide your own as if it was all a joke and hopefully somehow this will be the breakthrough to confidence – irony is always a good hiding place for lack of ability. That's when Boney M comes on.

Rasputin. Oh yes – you love this song – yep you're gonna do it - you're gonna try that move – the Russian Cossack spin you saw Boney M do on Top of the Pops as the drum and balalaika plays and down you go to the squat, fold your arms, drop onto your haunches and kick those legs – then make the leap and ask the short-haired brunette in the skin-tight blue neon thing and...

You're down. On the floor, confused – quick get up - your leg gave out and you quickly realise those Russian dancers were like – well - real dancers who practised and everything. The short haired girl in skin-tight neon blue takes a glance and moves on with her silver-heeled friends, Tony, in his loose yet well fitted cream suit, helps you up.

'What the hell you thinking?'

'Can we leave?'

But Malcolm, slightly older with a car and real girlfriend exudes confidence.

'Nice one Kenneth - let's a get a drink.'

Terry, now minus the gold dress girl, but forever the clubber in the loose suit and progressive rock hairdo let's himself go as ever, dances as if he's already forgotten who he was with. Tony – effortlessly stylish, are all in their own worlds – moving as if they're enjoying this – and you don't get it how their limbs move with the rhythm, the beat. Only you and Mark remain watching, but he won't be for long. This dancing is a mystery and one that defies anything you studied in 'O' level Physics. The heels get closer, you half turn, just in case. They realise you've noticed their temporary navigational error and oh so painfully and almost imperceptibly turn their heels by a carefully calculated ten degrees away from you, then another ten, then fifteen – then 45 and yep, they're now dancing with their backs to you. But they've noticed, they've noticed I exist, so maybe later, when the slowies come on, maybe then...

And that's one of the things you love about this place – the potential.

Malcolm says it's time to regroup, so, exhausted you head purposefully and with confidence back to the safety of the shining glossy bar with the mind of a prize fighter limbering up for the big match as the purple neon blinds you in the mirrored bar backdrop, you order another Pernod.

'Let's face it...' says Malcolm, Sue joins him from the floor, her smiling face reassures you that not all women are the enemy 'you ain't gonna score tonight.' She shakes her head in agreement.

Tonight? How about ever? Yet the overbearing truth punches you deep below the belt and you gasp for air – which comes out as Indignance, feigned surprise, you'll show him, just as soon as you're left alone and the right track comes on – not this one – definitely not 'Three Times a Lady'. No, given the right track, the right moment, the right girl... like that standing on a tree ledge...

'If you don't jump you can't be in the gang'.

And all afternoon you sat on the ledge of that tree, unable to plummet fifteen feet to the soft leaf mould of Bluebell woods. Yet another gang you'd happily been hanging out with who eventually come to a dare you couldn't or wouldn't do. Why can't there be a gang for cowards who can do everything else perfectly fine? Is this gang going to desert you?

The slowies announce themselves without warning – 'And thanks, for the times, that you've gi-ven me – the memories are all in my mind...' and you're frantic

– you walk purposefully past 'scared of nothing' Terry who's already heading for the floor, arm around his trophy in white heels and orange permed hair, past Malcolm and Sue the couple, you see Tony –

'Wanna drink?'

'Nah – here goes.'

You're left standing as your trusted wingman in your little club on inaction takes the lead and goes in for the kill on the blonde flowing hair one. Deserted and in full view of the bar and fellow friends. Quick, keep moving, do not stare into that vast space where girls avoid your eyes – and they always have friends to talk to – they don't seem to care whether someone asks them or not. So, you head for the toilets, it's the only hope. You head for the cubicle and throw the seat down, luckily it's not covered in piss so you happily take a seat and momentarily reflect on your inability to join the human race. Surely it'll get better.

Outside, the Commodores drift painfully on like a slow torture, and you fully know that when this one finishes another will strike up – and what then? Stay here for the next twenty minutes? Is there anywhere else? Why did you come here? What are you doing? Have you stooped this low that you're hiding in the toilet in 1979? Is this what being 18 is all about? Surely this means you're in need of help – who hides in the toilet in a disco? You ponder the cigarette butt floating in the bowl, examine the flood of urine lapping at the rims of your lace ups and wonder how you avoid this ever happening again. Outside the door, the flimsily locked cesspit of safety, outside the challenge of the music drifts by in lost opportunity.

Finally… finally you wander out sheepishly and Terry's at the bar having had one dance and moved on; luckily disco friends are still happy to talk and it stops them breaking one of the key rules – never be seen on your own. You mumble something about your stomach; communication is mostly sign language as the faster songs kick in again and you happily get back on the floor having regained your mates, some with new found women which you casually move among as if you know them - as if you're Woody Allen in Play It Again Sam and want to communicate this funny idea to Tony - but he's too busy dancing with the girl he asked. Which means you're on your own again, which also means you might do the same, one night, maybe some of what he's got will rub off.

5,4,3,2,1 Happy New Year!

'1980. It's a new decade' says Tony. Sound of popping, tinsel falls, arms round necks, random kissing of girls, you half expect to suffer the same from this level of sudden anarchy.

It dawns on you too. The 60s were half your life, the 70s were school; but the 80s?

Eventually you find yourselves all staring out to the floor as the last die-hards hang on to their new-found love of their lives of the last two hours, most of whom they'll never see again in the frenzy of lost or made up numbers; they desperately snog, feel, fondle in the need to find a mate, whilst we somehow take in the sounds, the smell of spilled beer, until Malcolm, our leader with a car and a real girlfriend, mercifully says:

'We going then?'.

And we all breathe a sigh of relief and once again you have something purposeful to do – like queue for coats – which is the closest you've got to a girl all night as the short haired brunette waits in front of you with bangles, earrings and the electric neon blue dress that ties at the sides, before all heading down with your ears ringing, thin brown lapels turned in to protect you from December's icy rain spatter, into the early morning air, where it's your turn in the boot and you reflect on another successful night – okay - this is just practise – but you'll get better. It's a twelve-foot assault course wall - but apparently, this is the only option if you want a girlfriend. There's no other way.

As you peer out backwards, you watch the red lights streaming past and the neon and the beautiful orange uniformed rows of towering motorway sentinels leading to other worlds as you ponder the advances made, the successful concealment of where you disappeared to for twenty minutes as George Benson asks everyone to 'Gimme the Night' and as your road drifts up from the motorway and the Cortina glides to a halt, you jump out with the usual wave of 'goobye', wander up the garden path before finding the key under the pot round the back, letting yourself in very slowly and trying to get over the stair that always creaks before throwing yourself between the sheets, ears still ringing and happy that you've seen the nightlife, you've lived at last, that she's out there somewhere, on that floor, just a few steps away...

2: Stayin' Awake.

Two days later, your ears are still ringing and you're *not* doing the Tony Manero walk with the paint pot and the Bee-Gees playing in the background down Brooklyn high street, but you *are* cycling that trusty yellow bike up that bastard hill and down the dual carriageway into the little suburban town called Fareham, where they've just got a Mall, ten miles from the Portsmouth metropolis; so this *could* be Brooklyn - at a stretch.

You spend the day sitting in a cubicle in a shirt, tie and the same black, moulded-sole lace-up shoes at the Unemployment Benefit Office; getting them to fill in the form UB410a and then discovering that the shaven-headed, angry claimant with 'Love' and 'Hate' tattooed on his knuckles (just out of prison) isn't going to get any benefit because he punched the boss and made himself unemployed so he doesn't qualify – and it's up to you to tell him the good news…

You sidle round the chair, 'Love and Hate' is all expectant and shaven-headed with you in your grey school jersey trying to break it to him slowly:

'Well sir – I'm afraid it's like this…'

So his cigarette is fired at you with a flick of his finger and sails past your left ear with the threat of it being followed closely by a fist, so you're left sitting at an empty cubicle as the rest of the shuffling unemployed nod at the one geezer giving it to the *man* – you – the boy in the school jersey – with the ears that are still ringing. You are the idiot for taking the job – last week you were in the queue like them – now you're less than them.

At your desk you have your box of unemployed claimants – people who need payment and some with no fixed abode who get it in cash – and 'Babs' the Boss is asking for volunteers at the weekend to deal with the backlog and all you can think of is what the 'B' side of 'Love Injection' says which goes 'Gone For The Weekend' which is right now your mantra and guide book to escape - a far cry from Tony Manero's paint shop – where he knew the boss and he gave him a raise and there were no shaven headed customers but quaint old ladies - and you wonder how can anyone keep this up, as you shake your head at her request and dread your pretended purposeful walk out in front of the queues, avoiding their eyes of accusation.

'Hey – weren't you here in the queue last week?' Says the guy with the eyebrows who lets his crumpled yellow UB40 fall on the desk for you to pick up and stamp with a little black dumbbell sign.

'Yep – that was me – thought I'd check out the other side'. But he shuffles off with a shrug before you've finished.

'So, I don't qualify for nuffin?'' exclaims the over-made up girl with the giant earrings, blood red lipstick and her giggling mates in tow. Could be her daughters...

'Sorry' is all you utter and she throws the pencil at the desk, it bounces up and bounces off your face. She storms out with a jangle of bracelets. You ponder the angry attractiveness; you also ponder how terrified you'd have been of her last night. Now here you are telling her 'no'. Why can't you be delivering paint in Brooklyn and is it Friday yet?

The audience sneer at your onstage performance as the evil prince – if it was a convention to hiss they would. Good on 'er' you feel them murmur. Once again you are 'the man'; the spineless face of authority, the weasel-featured government inspector we all want to avoid being. Not only that – you can't ask women to dance and can't dance yourself. Surely this is temporary, because soon you'll be away forever, leaving this sad, marking time existence

behind and gaining experience, confidence, stories...
because you have a plan...

3: We all become Millionaires.

Tuesday: Malcolm pulls up outside in the Cortina estate and you all pile out and quickly straighten your pastel-shaded Top Man jackets and push up the sleeves before entering the expectant darkness of the new joint called 'Street Level' which is written in neon purple, green, yellow and red tubes above the bar. The barmaid's wearing a bow tie and you note the Southampton sophistication – it's all very Malibu. If Portsmouth was New York, Southampton is L.A. and you glance around at the Kool and the Gang album cover clothing – loose jackets, ties even, deck shoes, belts hanging down; the women in baggy trousers that go tight at the waist and around the ankle. You sip your orange juice and talk about the music playing as you overload on the visuals after that day dodging cigarette butts. Just a few months now...

Sister Sledge pumps out the speakers as you unload the car once again and queue outside Southampton's hottest ex-bingo hall, dickie bows stand guard as always; judging, sneering, reading your lack of money, lack of charisma, lack of age.

'How old we gotta be?'

'Twenty-One'

'How old do I look?'

'Fifteen'

'I'm seventeen Terry'

'You look younger'

'What about the shirt?'

Tony, looking this time as if he's straight off a Brother's Johnson album cover with a loose white jersey that heaven forbid, has no shirt or vest under it, offers essential advice that the teachers never mentioned. In this world of trendy visual codes, he confuses what makes him look cool with what you're wearing and, more importantly, who's wearing it... From the speakers, you hear 'Where 'life is the journey and love is the trip and the study of them will make you hip...'

'Hmm just...'

'What?'

'Undo the buttons or something...'

'It's supposed to make me look older.'

'Never mind.'

'Bet Travolta never had these problems.'

'He doesn't live in Fareham.'

'Well, sod it, if we can't get in we'll go to 'Fridays' instead.'

'We can't afford it – '

'Yeah because you spent all your money on that Yukimura LP.'

'Haruko Yamashita – it's a rare jazz classic.' You say Indignantly, because weekends at eighteen in the early 1980s was not what you'd think. The all-important meet-up was a trip to Southampton on the train followed by a swift walk down to St Mary's Road via Top Man looking at jackets we couldn't afford, before hitting the market stalls and backstreet indie record shops selling imports. It meant absolutely nothing then because you imagined every town had backstreet indie record shops; nowadays the street reflects the rest of the world, recently bulldozed with a few chain stores. No records, no indie shop, no import of Hiroshi.

How we would flip through those endless reams of 12-inch vinyl with their alluring picture promise of other worlds, but eventually you find that elusive import that happens to have arrived that morning and here it is before anyone else can lay their hands on it. Seven quid, the price of an LP and a day's work. Worth every penny.

The rest of the weekend is taken up with preparation for the evening, a microwaved burger that is strangely white hot on the inside despite the luke warm exterior taught us a sudden lesson in thermodynamics; train ride home, maybe a run before the Cortina estate arrives and the wormhole to a new galaxy opens.

The album cover featured a Japanese guy wearing an anorak and holding a trombone; we had no idea that you could be in the music scene and not want to look like George Benson in one of those jerseys without a shirt, but what was irrefutable was the quality of music that came out of that pissed-off Yamashita's trombone. How was this dude linked to all we'd listened to already? But it was. Disco was a door to jazz, soul, blues. piano lessons - and even Japanese trombonists.

Anyway, you walk out of Street Level's neon green cocktail glass above the black bar and into the damp air of London Road, pulling your thin lapels around your far too thin flannel shirt in a desperate attempt to survive the English winter and the journey to the Cortina, into the boot, before a one mile out of town to a housing estate and drive to the venue looking more like a B+Q hardware store, known as the Top Rank, otherwise known inspirationally as 'Millionaires' and the first stage of the assault course that might have you all falling at the first hurdle, because the first stage on your journey is to get past the mystical Greek monster that guards the cave, otherwise known as...

4: Obstacle Number One: The Bouncer.

You approach the door in the damp December evening and the all too familiar hand of the ex-Marine/Para'/Cage fighter makes the merest lift of his fingers which immediately signals that we stop. So, we stop. He's got a cut over his left eye which is badly stuck together with a plaster.

'Sorry gents - members only tonight.'

'Told you.'

So once again you suggest 'Fridays', but that's 'grab a granny' night (over twenty-fives) – do they still go to Discos at that age? - and if they do – why? Aren't they just settling down with children at that age? You ponder the inequality of a world that only lets in the beautiful people - like Studio 54 – so you're gonna have to get a better shirt, and those shoes need to go when you get the Christmas money.   You contemplate a night in 'Street Level' as you find yourself shuffling amidst Tony, Malcolm and Susie.

Then, suddenly you see Sarah.

You know Sarah from sixth form and you got to know her better during the Geography field trip – laughed at your jokes - and she once gave you her drink – it was Pernod and that's been your drink ever since.

'Isn't that -?'

'Yep.'

'Call her over – she's got membership.'

'No way.'

'You said you knew her.'

'I kinda do – don't stare.'

Luckily, the bouncer bars your way.

'Sorry sirs you need to join to become members.'

'How'd we join then?' The usual answer consists of having to be over 21, needing a special voucher that you didn't know about, and then being signed in by an existing member - which you don't know; in other words - forget it. Apart from the fact that the beautiful girl right in your line of vision you're trying to avoid eye contact with appears to be a member, could sign you in, could be a gateway to future discourse, could be, if you'd call out.

'Fill in a form over there' says the ex-Para' Disco Nazi. The cut looks painful.

'How much?' Await the figure that will reduce your long awaited second-hand car savings to zero.

'Free', mutters the bouncer with a tinge of embarrassment, like you're the last bunch of under-age urchins in Southampton to know that this isn't America, this is a small town that has no idea how to harness this teenage youth thing and start making money. Nope – that happened in the 90s. So, no need for the call out to Sarah. Hmm, just as well.

You even get a plastic card, wave them at the dickie-bowed border guard and the glass doors open, the velvet curtain falls aside, the stage awaits and the lights inside begin to sparkle as you enter a hall the size of a sports arena... a gladiatorial coliseum whose sole purpose is to enable peacocks to flaunt their moves and bag themselves the one with the tightest dress and biggest eyelashes. You look up...

The crowds hang over the balcony and watch the black West End Posse with their black T shirts, afros and the set dance routine, then there's the blonde model type who appears to be chaperoned by her mother and everyone avoids, there's the group of check-out girls in pencil skirts, gold high heels and thin gold belts whilst you glance at neon green, purple, yellow as that tanned short-haired brunette with the body suddenly parades past you, laughing, in the skin-tight neon blue thing with the sides tied in knots like that album cover as Earth, Wind and Fire set the mood to the velvet hammer of a bass line:

'Midnight creeps so slowly into hearts of men who need more then they get...'

and you watch as they merge on the battleground and start a set of moves that you will never figure out.

Then the staccato clickety clickety click of the lead guitar signals the start up and...

Silver heels flash, strings erupt, blue lurex and coffee flesh as the piano hits three notes and 'said upside down you're turnin' me and drifting purple skirt, neon yellow diagonal cut amidst green lazer - givin' love instinctively – round and round you're turnin' me – Diana Ross to Nile Rogers' distinctive click as the bangles glint and short blonde hair bounces whilst long brown – piano dum dum – such a simple bass and yet just off the beat – boy you turn me – inside out – and – round and round – New York is right here in front of you and these girls out in their best Tuesday night and you're not sure you care as it's a relationship between you and Diana right now and her cutting diva voice as you let the sound take you far away from the beige and grey of the dole office and into the Miami pastels. You've lost the last five minutes – and – round and – round – there's Nile on guitar - kicking in at the end – yep they're playing the twelve inch - keep going – heels flash, hair brushes, the posse is in town doing their routine with the four black dudes and the T shirts 'Southampton Soul

Patrol' and right now we're all in this together understanding how we're meant to live life like the surfer riding the top of a wave - yep – take it away Nile.

To say there were many differing styles of dancers in 1979-80 is something of an understatement:

1: 'Gestapo glasses':

Named after the Maths teacher and dressed like one with giant Herbie Hancock frames; he would start by leaning casually against a pillar in Granny's, watching out over the floor, sipping from a tumbler, quietly adjusting his large-framed glasses with a poke of the index finger every few minutes. Suddenly the decision was made – he was going to DANCE and it was mayhem. Couples needed to sidestep this flailing phenomenon until, just as quickly as he started, he stopped – in one step he was back by the pillar sipping at his tumbler, adjusting his glasses and nodding.

2: The 'Funker':

Had all the right gear, hair over one eye in the style of Phil Oakey style whilst fully adopting the tucked in ski jumper, baggy pleated jeans, deck shoes and hanging-down belt of the 'soul boy' fraternity; he would move side to side – right to the left – left to the right – throughout the night. Sometimes he might do a slow 360 degree turn, never pulled, just kept his head down, doing his thing - he seemed happy.

3: The 'Big Buckled Bastard':

So named because his checked shirt, bad haircut, awkward demeanour and oh yes - his massive belt buckle. He'd lean back and the narrow shoulders would begin the rolling motion as the elbows took up the rhythm like some kind of Status Quo fan gone Country Western, dancing to Disco's inner country-western beat.

On rare occasions, all three of the above characters got together, took over a corner of the floor and just 'went for it' in a display of flailing, side stepping, big buckled status quo-inspired disco mayhem. Of course, at the back of your mind you know that despite their shortcomings, at least they have the balls to get up there and let go.

4: The 'Ninja':

Dressed in black flowing silk – which was what all the 'Kung Fu' students wore in Gosport and Fareham at the time – he'd be going through his set series of moves whilst trying to dance to the music; it could be quite good to see his interpretation of Donna Summer's 'I Feel Love' to the White Crane style of

Martial Art, but of course this did inevitably lead to some heavy geezer at the side of the floor pointing, laughing and generally taking the piss amidst the plastic silver palm trees. The skinny, black clad figure kept on as if he didn't notice, sticking to his moves and working his way through his set series of actions. More piss taking, the mates are joining in, the figure lifts his leg to adopt another stance but instead of continuing the move he lets out one beautifully executed side thrusting kick to the stomach of the heckler - in time to the music - who then doubles up, knocking the wind out of his lungs and the beer out of his hand, as he falls back into a seated position on the floor and remains doubled up. His mates try to help him up but he can't talk, he's gasping for air as he is eventually picked up and carried away. The bouncers didn't notice what happened but realise *something* had just happened. The Ninja carries on dancing without breaking rhythm.

5: Obstacle Number Two: The Dancefloor.

So you sheepishly wander in to Millionaires – which is a giant black painted hall with red velvet and glitter balls all over the place otherwise known as the Top Rank Ballroom Suite and It's a big space so you and Tony can hide much easier as Susie hits the floor with Malcolm, and you watch with curious envy at someone with a regular girlfriend living the life you'll one day experience; but in the meantime, you sip your Pernods and observe the thousand beautiful people for once all knowing where to go on a Tuesday night. There's still a sense of festivity, party, excuse for fun as you discover this alternate reality from the daily queue of claimants which feels like at least a week ago now… and there's Sarah – Sarah Craig. But to ask her would be madness, pointless, suicidal. So, you wait.

'They're gonna come to you, are they?' Thanks Terry. But you know he's right.

'Eventually.'

You clearly haven't convinced and he wanders away to mix with past flames and acquaintances, this really isn't your world at all. It's as if you have to flaunt and spread your peacock feathers in a show of dancing skill, but this is all there is – if you can't succeed here you cannot succeed with women... full stop. So, you keep watching, observing, trying to learn a way in, trying to spot a common thread as to why these girls seem to know something you don't.   You turn and ask for another orange juice as Tony returns from the floor.

'I said hip, hop, a hipp-it...' comes over the speakers

'What the hell's this?'

'Sugarhill Gang – called 'rap'.

'More like crap'.

'That ain't gonna catch on - look at her Tony – she's everything we're not.'

You point at the album cover stuck to the wall – the photo of a dark beauty in an electric blue dress leans against a railing in palm tree, blue sky paradise looking out over the oasis in post disco reverie – suggesting an exotic world far away even from here - her hair blown by the pacific breeze, you feel like you'd get on – if only you knew her. But, you're here – Southampton Top Rank in January 1980 and she's probably a cool New Yorker, dancing in Studio 54, or out there on Venice Beach at least three thousand *light years* away. Never in your lifetime.

'She's a model.'

Yeah maybe, but she's more than that, she's disco – saying to me - come on...this is the life you've been waiting for! I'm out here guys just come and get me. Blueness of Santa Monica sun in the background, the sequins glisten in the magic hour as her smooth limbs show you a world of what could be. Amidst the band name written in that upbeat, leaning forward font (why doesn't everyone use that?) she says – this is what's out there and she's aware of a better place... the album cover is... Southampton on a Tuesday night.

That's your ideal, but right now you need to start your apprenticeship.

'Yeah – in your dreams.' Tony mutters exactly what you're both thinking.

You both know that maybe it's true and he'd probably have more luck than you given the circumstances because he'd come across more down to earth whilst you'd be grovelling at her feet like the eighteen-year old who's never been out of Fareham that you are, with your Tuf shoes and the checked shirt that's beginning to fray at the collar.

'Oops up-side your head - said oops upside your head...' is suddenly all around you as The Gap Band heralds a phenomenon of the time. As if on cue, the entire floor sits down with legs wide apart and

interlocks arms to do the dance called the 'row boat'
in lines and lines of pleated gold trousers, deck shoes,
ski jerseys and sweaty cheesecloth and Tony says let's
go and you don't know any better and so – though
the warning signs are there - you follow and you're
amongst feet and towering awkwardly amongst disco
people all sat interlocked rocking their arms and going
through an easily followed sit down dance routine
and in comes the bass and you think that maybe you
should know the person better who's legs you back
up against – and you feel awkward and have had no
time to practice so your movements come off stunted
and out of rhythm and you find yourself at the front –
the last in line – facing the crowd – the crowd of
watchers you would right now rather be with but
have committed and are therefore having to carry on
the rowing boat movements and you begin to realise
that the guy sat down facing you with his requisite
blonde girlfriend is mouthing 'wanker' – that how you
feel is being transmitted word for work into his vision
and is now being used as a weapon of psychological
destruction as you half-heartedly lean left, lean right,
hands up, clap, clap, lean left, lean right, hands above
- clap, clap. You try to follow but all you hear to the
beat is 'I'm a wanker - I'm a wanker' clap, clap directly
in front of you.

You laugh, desperately trying to pretend you're
laughing at the whole event, but you, he and his

girlfriend all know the joke is you, in your five-year old lace up shoes, trousers with untrendy belt, shirt that's been washed too many times and that bastard brown jacket. Mercifully the Gap Band fade out and you quickly get up and head for the crowd as the DJ announces that we'd just made the record for the biggest row boat dance anywhere in the country. So, what, it wasn't good for you.

You decide to follow Tony's lead and you shout your order of Two Orange juices and Lemonades - please - in the same glass (She mishears) Not one big glass, in separate glasses (she motions confusion) Okay, one Orange Juice and lemonade in the same glass, followed by another Orange juice and lemonade, also in another glass (She nods, clearly wondering) Yes, two Orange juices and lemonades. Separate glasses.

You turn to Tony and hand him the drink which is beginning to taste like the acid it is and comment on the barmaid who wears a black waistcoat and seems distracted from all the action and therefore somehow above it – like the overseer of all the desire surrounding her.

'She's nice'.

'You think?'

'Then ask her'

'Ask her what?'

'if she wants a drink'

'You reckon?'

'Why not? She looked at you'.

'Did she?'

Two more drinks arrive - why? She looks at you as if you just yelled abuse – you nod 'okay', wave compliance, pour the two drinks into your existing drinks, understand what happened, pay the double round and in a moment of cavalier disregard for your weekly pay packet shout your generous question of whether she wants a drink, whilst leaning across the bar and nicely dowsing your jacket sleeves deep in the cocktail of spilled cheap beer and sticky rose that covers the glossy black top. She looks back at you with beautifully arched eyebrows and heightened theatrical response. In the disco, all responses have to be theatrical because you cannot afford mistaken messages. What you've just done is the school-boy error of classic mistaken message – you should have leant over with a massive confident smile having gained her attention by waving your hand at her – then raised both eyebrows with a wry turn of the mouth to suggest 'wise guy but what the hell' and then, only then, say 'hey' – pointing at the drink – 'why not have one for yourself? – I'm buying...'

(women always look better when mildly annoyed – maybe that's why they make their eyebrows that shape). So, not surprisingly she shouts with a well-spoken, beautifully clipped, mild annoyance of the college girl crossing the border to speak to you – 'I'm sorry?'

'I said - why don't you have one for (pointing) your – self!'

'Why don't I – what?

You repeat one more time and she gets the message and you watch her eyes suddenly look at you in surprise, consider the absurd prospect of a potential date, then dismiss you as ridiculous all in three seconds of facial judgment. Your insane offer has caused her shock, incredulity and swift denial all expressed in the space of two words:

'Er – no'.

Ever there at the kill, Tony asks 'How'd you feel'. It's not a question.

6: Obstacle Number Three: Asking the Girl of Your Dreams.

You tell him you don't care and remind him that his forays onto the dancefloor have also come to nothing; to which he replies that he's 'in' and he's just in the process of buying her a drink. You're shocked, you rely on neither of you ever getting a steady girlfriend - which guarantees your safety on the dancefloor side-lines by always having a mate to hang out with whilst everyone else has regular lives with girls and future and semi-detached houses; but that's not for you. You're clearly going to have to be the guy who achieves elsewhere – by being a Soldier. Then Discos will be a joke – you'll wander in with a swagger – having scaled walls and fired guns and run up beaches; how could a disco not be just like visiting the old-school playground after that? Women will fall at your feet, and all you have to do is things you find easy – like climbing and running – absolutely no rhythm or false showing off required, not involving dance or art or anything in any way creative…

You ponder your future as the opening chords of 'September' strike up and a sudden flow to the floor begins as another electric blue dress brushes past.

You nudge Tony as he leans over the bar, missing the spilt beer and ordering a Vodka and Coke.

So - you got condoms?

What you on about?

Condoms? Do you have them?

'No – why?'

'Better be ready.'

'What – you mean - Isn't that a little bit hopeful?'

'Not really - it'll all happen so quickly.'

'Yeah but –'

'– next thing you know...'

Followed by a furtive, shouted discussion as to how many are required, assessing the possibility of one breaking and then that being it – disaster – career, future, Athena print lifestyle – all gone for good and replaced by a pushchair and a council estate – followed by yourself climbing onto Southampton's equivalent of the Brooklyn Bridge where you throw yourself off in a suicidal cry for help because your mates aren't really listening...

'– anyway, machines are in the toilets...'

Tony sips the juice and looks out over the sparkly, blackened hall of revolving purple lights;

'The guy didn't jump'.

'Didn't he?'

'No'

'Wasn't he trying to do a handstand?'

'It was because his girlfriend was pregnant and his mate wouldn't listen.'

You both ponder the climax of Saturday Night Fever, trying to remember what exactly happened to Bobby C after he drove from the gang-fight.

'if he had made sure she was on the pill in the first place'.

'So, would you still wear condoms if she was on the pill?'

You reply without pause – 'Of course'. Tony quickly sips his orange juice and does a double take;

'She'd be on the pill and you'd use two condoms?

You nod and murmur 'yeah' sheepishly, because you know you would, if you ever get the chance.

'I cannot deny – that is safe sex.' You both return to

your Orange Juices whilst you rapidly scan the floor for possible hopefuls because any moment now your faithful partner in ineffective disco dating is going to disappear into the wilderness of coupledom, leaving you lonely, nervous, and lost...

And then you spot her again; Sarah from school, in a white dress.

It must have been at least a year. You tell Tony not to look now so he spins round on his heels, catching her eye immediately, tells you that 'weak heart never caught fair maiden', which somehow seems to have credibility because it sounds grand.

'Stop looking at her, she'll guess.' You get frantic. Too late.

'Hang on she's looking - go on then wave - you're the one who knows her.'

'- only from class.'

'That's a start.'

'Yeah but I never talk to her. Stop waving, will you?'

'Hang on – she's looking – go on then wave – you're the one who knows her.'

'We just had a chat on the Geography field trip'

'She's coming over – look - maybe she just wants a chat.'

'With me?'

Her face is one big smile of teeth like they have in films. You can just hear her beautifully clipped enunciation through the music.

'Didn't know you were a fan of Disco, Kenneth.' Her beam continues, so unreal it's painful. You feel a mix of racing excitement and complete loss of control as you turn to find the exotic Malaysian-like eyes, short brown hair and a smile that is way above your punching weight, a smile that you know will propel her to other cities, countries and other relationships with expensive husbands - if it hasn't already. You are still dazzled by the radiance of the teeth and haven't even got to taking in the way she's dressed before you realise she's spoken and is awaiting a reply. Naturally you've gulped a mouthful of Coke and your attempt to speak at the same time results in the fizzy liquid going straight up your nasal cavity and exploding from your tear ducts...

'Oh dear – are you okay?'

You splutter and remain faced with an exotic, overpowering album cover beauty right in front of you - who is actually talking – and talking to you – yes you.

'I'm fine – hello Sarah – sorry'.

She ignores your disablement and keeps in the swing of the moment, because she's going places, far from here, but right now she's with you, passing by, like the QE2 en-route to New York via Lee on Solent, and right now you are the old penny arcade on the seafront, waving forlornly at the multi-tiered decks – of her teeth.

'So, you guys dancing?'

Yes, let's play that game, let's pretend we're someone different - are we dancing? What does she mean? We're just taking a rest from a perfectly normal and successful night at the disco and it is essential we get this right because one false move and HMS Sarah Craig will pass by in all her resplendence to lands and shores further afield and –

'Er…' and then the wild card…

'*You* two go dance – I've got to deliver these drinks' says Tony and you look at him like he's just turned into a mad demon. He throws you a glance and walks away with his drinks leaving you suspended on a tight rope without a safety net, perched with a thousand foot drop as the hope of something happening slowly dawns on you – you might be able to make it to the other side of the canyon. You turn to face her – no way – don't be silly. Bastard Tony – a thoughtless gesture to drop you into the impossible scenario of spending time with Her – you cannot win – so accept defeat and get out, make your excuses before you embarrass yourself and fall into the deep canyon and lose the magic; because right now, if you can walk away unblemished, unrefused, this has suddenly become one helluva night. Just don't push it...

She's looking – expectantly – why? Because she is expecting to be asked.

You feign nonchalance – that'll work.

'What – to this'?

'Don't mind if you don't want to'.

Yeah that's right, just refuse your million-dollar cash prize, just wave it away. Because you know only too well that this is the moment you'll lose her, if only you could just stay talking, looking, smiling, without any need to do anything physical – because then she'll discover...

'It's not that – it's just this is a little awkward to dance to'.

Stayin' Alive – BeeGees – you kidding? The most danceable track in the Universe? But the record isn't fun anymore, the music is an assault course of secret movements that must be completed correctly or face ridicule, shame, loss of ego-boosting beautiful company.

'Okay – maybe another time then.'

Your free Lamborghini Countach has revved its engine and is about to drive away forever. So you throw yourself in front of its front spoiler and hope for the best.

7: Obstacle Number Four: Dancing.

'Let's do it.'

You impress yourself with your macho determination and hope it'll impress her whilst leading her out onto the floor that opens up like you're now escorting an ocean-going liner into Southampton docks – but this time you're on board – and you're gliding past the handbags and the heels and the swishing of bodies and the crimplene and the nylon and the odd flare and the flashing and flickering and if only you could just keep walking with her to – somewhere else like – like a room with a bar that was quiet and a TV – but you know you have to stop. You know you - should - be - dancing. Yeah. Hmm.

It's like waking from a dream where you fall in love that in fact it was true and you are in love – and there she still is – having somehow not been grabbed by some hulk on the way onto the floor – still facing you with that smile. She's already moving without any effort, so far, she doesn't know, maybe she'll never know, maybe you can pull this off. Maybe her beauty and coolness have inspired you to greater things, maybe you'll never have to worry about this again, you've breached the watershed of adulthood, the barrier has been surmounted. You will now find love, happiness, marriage, children, holidays and a house with smoke glass windows and a decent Ford Capris; In the frenzy of the moment you start dancing along with her effortless movement and it is then that you begin to realise, the Lambo' has driven right over your poor, useless body as she leans in, perfect teeth, brown almond eyes and a bead of sweat on her forehead under the spiked brow of her short brown hair and utters the words that still shatter your dreams:

'Where did you learn to dance like that?'

No, she's not in awe...the ship crashes into the harbour, the Lambo' reverses back over your crushed pelvis which has now been out in traction; you're back where you were five minutes ago – tragically normal – unsure of yourself – you've forgotten that you couldn't swim and here you are in the deep end; but this is no swimming pool, you're out at sea without a raft or lifejacket in this whirlpool of gyrating disco dancers with all their bangles, heels, tight dresses tied at the sides, big hair, cheesecloth shirts, handbags on the floor, and right now you're trying very hard to move with a relaxed sense of bending knees, drop shoulders – relax – it'll get better...

So, you go for humour as you answer her question;

'New York – this is all the rage out there'.

'It's different'.

'What's different?'

'Your legs are all – kinda stiff - is that a New York thing?'

Yeah that's a big New York thing.'

'Looks kinda – I dunno – funny.'

'They laughed at Elvis to start with.'

'Did they?'

'I did'.

'You look kinda like – a robot.'

'It's based on robotics.'

'Oh - can you do robotics?'

'Anyone can – just precision that's all.'

'Wow - Go on then.'

And with that very encouragement – akin to Farrah Fawcett Majors inviting you to a late-night party with the rest of Charlie's Angels in their flat-share on Sunset Boulevard - you quickly take the bait and consider that maybe the Lambo isn't going to run over you after all; that maybe you're going to not only survive, but startle her, impress her, really show her something.

You have no idea where the energy comes from, but the adrenaline is running as the Bee Gees falsetto shouts 'stayin A-liiiiiiive' and you find yourself locking the arms, the head and suddenly moving in precise rigid, right-angled movements and you stare straight ahead with an almost uncanny robotic glazed look coming into your eyes – you ARE a robot, you ARE the definition of robotics.

'Wanker'. Yeah, him again, somehow it sounds above the music from the crowd on the floor where you've forced a small clearing. You pretend not to hear.

'Needs work but that's the general idea'.

'Okay'. All is going well, you can dance like a demon, she thinks you're cool.

'Funny – to start with I felt really nervous about dancing with you'.

'Really?'

'Yeah – but now I don't care – I can really let loose'. You feel like everyone else at last, joining the club of those that can 'love the nightlife' like Alicia Bridges. Right now, you're leaving the teenage years behind.

'Let's dance normally now'. You note the change in her tone and sense problems.

'Oh sure – get so used to American dancefloors'. Yes, you think now's the time to mention America.

'When were you there?'

Tricky one, because 'never' is the real answer, but that's suicidal – you were in Canada two years ago with an International Air Cadet Exchange but how is that a good thing in this disco? Right now, you are the disco, you are that Brooklyn paint-shop worker.

'Few years back – saved up the money'. You throw in a quick spin – you're on fire.

'No really – let's dance normally now'. That tone again. You watch the micro-features cross her one-time radiant smile and a look of slight confusion and concern alter her features. Your world gets smaller as you realise you forgot to keep reminding yourself...

You. Can't. Dance.

So, you go for distraction whilst trying to change the subject and hoping this will enable you to relax those knees.

'I mean it'.

'What?'

'Dance normally'.

Complete capitulation, defeat. You state in desperation; 'this is how I dance''.

'Bend your legs more'.

'I'm bending my legs'.

'Just relax'.

'I'm a rag doll!'   You realise you've almost screamed your defence, 'look I'm relaxed okay?'

You've lost all hope, Sarah becomes the enemy as your cover is blown and once again the alien disco crowd begins to lap at your heels like an encroaching tide; you find yourself on a little pinnacle of rock unable to reach the shore, the bar, the safety of Malcolm, cool Tony, slow-dance Terry and a ride home in the Cortina estate.

'Well I better get back to my friends' she makes her excuse – 'thanks for the – for the – well – thanks anyway'.

'Look I can't dance – okay – I can do other stuff'.

And the tide finally washes over, engulfs and takes you down into the depths of unknown waters. You watch her sail away into the distant tropics of rich partners and unknown experience as she disappears into the crowd forever and Tony appears from nowhere – dancing with his new-found woman in a cheesecloth dress and long blonde hair.   Bloody hell.

'What was I supposed to do?'

'Never do robotics in front of a girl'.

Noted, five minutes too late.

Always be moving, so you retreat to the toilet, wipe the seat and think about why on earth you put yourself through this.   Why the urge to participate in an arena you clearly aren't designed for, where did all this start?

8: First Encounters

You remember your first one. 1974, the school hall, chairs stacked along the sides, a few paper plates with sausages on sticks, girls stand in a group and have a few dances with themselves; boys stand about wondering what the hell to do next, drink more Tizer, eat the crisps, cross the floor with purpose and make sure no one thinks you're dancing or asking anyone to dance. Eventually the lights are turned down and you can hide in the dark corners with your long empty plastic beaker, be slightly in awe of the girls as they seem to have no problem having a dance with their friends. A couple of 'lads' have the insane stupidity to walk out and start dancing – with the girls! – you all laugh at them – and then stop when you realise they're now dancing with the girls you secretly fancy and for some reason, look more attractive tonight and they seem to be enjoying themselves, whilst you all carry on sheltering in the corner, seemingly ignored by the girls, not quite knowing what you're supposed to do next. Then it's late, parents start arriving, you wander out, unlock your bicycle, put the dynamo on, cycle back to the Greendale estate. Mum calls out from the sitting room:

'Did you have a good time?'

'Yeah – thanks.'

'Good – did you dance?'

'Sorry?'

'Did you have a dance?'

'Er – no – not really.'

What she meant of course was - did you meet anyone like you were expecting to? So, my answer was an immediate admission of failure. I had no idea.

A few years later, whilst Steve Rubell was running the legendary Studio 54 in New York, turning away anyone rich or poor who didn't look 'good', you and Tony had The Plessey Social Club on the outskirts of Fareham – a small prefab building containing a bar, a table tennis room behind frosted glass and a bunch of one-armed bandits and pinball machines - where a group of middle aged men would prop up the bar and fill the machines with ten pence pieces, Tony would sign you in and you'd have table tennis on a Tuesday night, a disco on a Friday and pinball if you had any spare coins.

Of course, you never had any money, you always had essays to write for those A levels, you never got off with any women – but you had hope – it was bound to all work out in the end – the right girl, the falling in love, the house. It was a room with a bar and a floor of pissed up workers having a cheap pint and several cigarettes after the week's labour on lathes that became the hunting ground of 16-17 year olds trying to get served – and succeeding. It was here you had a go on your mate's 50cc, laid down in the wet road after too much cider and fell in love with the mystical world that seemed to develop its own rules after hours; that threw you into bar-side conversations with older locals. You also found out about drink as a mood changer - ordering a round as a gesture of friendship to a suddenly aggressive drunk and discovered how an evening could turn... always optimistic Terry noted that Sam – one of our school acquaintances – was at the bar leant over his drink:

Terry: Hey that's Sam at the bar.

Tony: Yeah but he's pissed.

We all knew what that tended to mean with Sam. Even at Seventeen.

Terry: I'll just say hello.

Tony: I wouldn't. He's pissed.

Terry wanders over. I don't look and immerse myself in the latest Space Invaders which they have on a desktop.   Terry wanders back.

Terry: He just hit me.

Tony: Told you.

We avoided Sam when he drank.

Then it would be back home for bread and peanut butter at half-midnight. Despite these humble beginnings and an inability to dance with any women, you felt things would soon improve once you escaped and did brave, physical things; that one day you'd be cruising in an electric blue Porsche 911 with Quincy Jones, George Benson and the Dude playing over the speakers. It was just a matter of time.   But first you had to get past the biggest obstacle of all...

9: Obstacle Number Five: The Slow Dance

You soon realise you and Tony are dancing kind of together, so you stop, Tony turns back to his blonde, you remain still amongst all the jostling bodies and quickly feel out of place at the bottom of the ocean with the sharks and shoals of Angel fish in the Aquarium; so you walk purposefully towards the bar like a heavily weighted deep sea diver navigating between the handbags and wondering what you're going to do when you get there, when suddenly those three dreaded piano notes echo around the floor and one big sigh seems to emanate from the crowd - it's time to get off the floor and seek the shelter of the bar. How you hate 'Three Times a Lady'.

Tony appears at your side.

'Off you go then'.

You feign ignorance, but he knows your excuses too well; why can't you be left alone to spectate? What's wrong with spectating? Standing on the side like some observer of the spectacle – like Toulouse Lautrec – why can't you? Are you not similarly disabled? He was short, you can't dance. It seems you are either a coward, or on the floor strutting about like some Lion finding your mate; no in between, just a jungle. Nature, in all its ruthlessness.

'Go and ask her to dance.' There she is all short brunette hair and that smile.

'Just have.'

'No – she asked you. Now you ask her for a slow dance.'

'Are you kidding? Just let me be happy with what I've got so far. Maybe I'll try - next week.'

'Maybe she won't be here next week'.

'Maybe she will…'

'She'll have met somebody else by next week.'

You know he's right. A week is a long time in disco land. On Saturday, you can be snogging like long time lovers – tongues and everything – and by next week you're not even acknowledging their presence. You know because you've seen this sort of thing going on, not to you, but, well…

'You think?'

'Go on – go seek fair maiden'.

All of sudden it's an Arthurian quest as you throw him a distracted glance of resignation, murmur 'bloody hell' and you're off marching toward her; she's half-chatting to another girl and half sees you out the corner of her cat-like eyes, you feel like you're about to fall over the cliff edge but you're committed and she looks at you and she knows because it's 'Three Times a Lady' and it's too late, but the look isn't inviting and why oh why do girls suddenly turn into this when you've walked the walk of at least twenty five metres going on half a mile and now you feel an idiot and haven't even asked yet, in your bloody Tuf lace up shoes that really shouldn't be worn in a disco you come to attention like a bloody air cadet and chin up, announce your intention to cross Antarctica by foot (which would be slightly easier):

'So–would-you-like-to-dance, then?'

'No thanks'.

'Okay'.

So, you make the long walk home, convinced of what you knew all along. What on earth were you thinking? Pushed it too far.

'What she say?'

'No'

'Why?'

'Dunno'

'Well didn't you ask?' You shuffle past to the bar to hide in the purpose of ordering a lemonade. You're exhausted and not in the mood for mission debrief.

'I thought that was enough' you try not to look too disappointed and scan the horizon for other fish so that she can see what kind of womanising go-getter you are, just before you move on to the next lucky lady.

'So, why'd she just been dancing with you?'

'Pity?'

'It's gotta be more than that...' you stare at Tony incredulously in that linen jacket that fits him like he's a grown up; he's kind of right, but how can you leap over that cliff again – those rocks hurt and this is descending from failure to ridicule as you march across the floor once again to ask her 'why', and she shouts nicely in your ear-with a smile and a whiff of 'Charlie' perfume - that she'd promised her *boyfriend* – in the Navy of course - that she wouldn't slow dance with anyone.

So, what is it about the Royal Navy around here? Are these sailors sat around in Pompey docks having some wild night out where they carry off most of the 17-year-old female population of Fareham, Southampton and Portsmouth put together? Press-ganged into motherhood and waiting for the ship's return in

Gosport before we could get to know them. Not fair. You react with relief at the refusal; job done, dare taken, refusal obvious.

'Oh – right – seeyah then'. March back purposefully, no strut needed, you're on solid ground, and like a returning jungle explorer who's just faced a Bengal Tiger and found it quite friendly after all. You tell Tony about the boyfriend. It's over. Like you ever had a chance. But Tony's got other plans…

'So? What's she dancing with you for if she's got a boyfriend?'

You don't really know – Curiosity? Friendship? Politeness? The mystery of women maybe? … all you know it was a 'No'. You're not going back out there – you are bloodied and scratched and lean back with the air of a veteran of the Disco Conflict era of '79-'80. They should hand out medals.

'So, try something else.' He can't possibly be serious.

'It's fine – really – she was nice about it'.

'You give up too easily'.

Mark pitches up with a loud Hawaiian shirt, ever on the look-out, head darting about wanting to know the score, confrontational, leaning forward, you tell him before he asks:

'I asked her - so there.'

'You actually asked her?'

'I actually asked her.'

'But she turned you down.'

'True – but It's progress.'

'You seeing her again?'

'No need.'

'What do you mean'?

'No need.'

'What does that mean?'

'Alright, if you must know - I danced like a twat.'

'Another drink then?' He takes pity.

'Yeah, what the hell – but make it an Orange Juice – I haven't earned a drink.'

Tony leans back against the bar in the thin lapelled jacket with the burgundy shirt, cream trousers and thin-soled shoes positively made for the nightlife, clothes you know you couldn't wear even if you could afford them, surveys our status and forecasts another night of lonely wannabe clubbers failing in their primary aim. Is this how life's going to be? How long will this continue?

And there it is – suddenly furious and strenuous activity means the nightly fight has broken out at the right-hand corner of the floor... girls keep dancing, two guys with bouffant hair and disordered pastel suits are escorted effortlessly to the doors almost in rhythm with the beat of H.A.P.P.Y, and creates a strange mix of cool Miami vice fashion mixed with aggressive pissed-up English yobbo. They disappear very efficiently, red faces and torn shirts.

'So, who shall we break the heart of next?' Mutters Tony.

His new bird 'Anna' has disappeared. You decide he needs cheering up. 'You can do better – she had a big nose – and we have the whole of Southampton out there.'

'You think?'

'Sure, plenty more where that came from.'

You both look around at the sheer flashing neon yellow and tropical orange beauty of this club, the silver trees, the gold pillars, the wildly rotating lights of purple, the impromptu dance teams, the beered up lads shouting in their in their tropical shirts, the flailing of limbs, the sub-woofer kicking out the slap bass of Mark King and it doesn't matter whether you're gonna ask her or not right now – you're here, you're amongst the handbags, the heels, the hair, the neon, the bass, and you never want to leave – you always want to be able to return to this – this thing – this 'Nightlife'.

'A city of many stories...

'Many dreams...'

'In the meantime - another night without any women.' That mythical, mysterious beast that is becoming further and further distant with every trip to the disco.

Suddenly the opening bars of 'September' sound from the double barrelled Boses and the floor begins to fill again as you listen to the lyrics as if they might offer a clue, some hope, a pathway... but Tony disagrees with you; is it 'Do you remember the twenty first night in September' or is it – as you know it is – 'The very FIRST night in September'? It's important you get this right because you need to know when the party is supposed to be - thereby signifying the end of August and the start of the darker nights, because what could the twenty first signify? Why say that? What clue is there in there for us in Portsmouth from the philosophical genius that is Maurice White and Earth Wind and Fire? Is there not a message for us in the lyrics? We need clues from such sages – just tell us what to do with the next fifty years please.

'So why not ask her if she wants a drink?' You tell him you don't know, he suggests you offer to buy her a drink, you cannot fathom his level of self-belief being thrust at you; self-belief cannot be just conjured up so – bloody hell... really? You start walking back *again*, the absurdity of your criss-crossing the same floor three times is not lost on you.

She looks round, mildly irritated? You're not sure, but you're also not sure if you care anymore.

'Would you like another Pernod?'

'Thanks, I'm okay'.

'Right – okay'. You're about to march off for the last time but she touches your rolled-up sleeve with her immaculately manicured hand – it might as well be the touch of a Nepalese Princess. A deity has touched your sleeve. Contact!

'Er – look - can I ask you a question?'

Progress, she's taking a personal interest in you and wants to know more; despite the boyfriend and all hopes of future marital bliss with this short-haired icon of beauty crashing and burning around you, the male persona remains strangely, foolishly resilient and hopeful, as if nothing had been said and she was contemplating throwing it all away for you – charismatic, robotic disco dancing, you... you brim with confidence and feel the night surging ahead; suddenly the music isn't your enemy. But there's only one question women ask you in those kind of circumstances – think about it – it can only be one thing - so it's time to play the digressive distracting game with a vengeance;

'Whatever it is the answer is yes' – your attempt at laddish humour is about 500 miles out.

'Oh' she says. Wrong.

Caught out by her sullen reaction you realise she hasn't caught on to your witty suggestion of you having interpreted the possible question as being whether you should spend the night together.

'Why, what were you going to ask?' You wince at the oncoming meteor, unable to dodge it...

'Are you a Virgin?'. Ding. You knew it.

'Hah!' You feign dismissal but it works about as well as your Tuf shoes saying 'smooth'.

'I just thought –

'I think I would be pretty worried if I hadn't – y'know – by now'.

'We're only eighteen'. Darn, could this have been a deep and meaningful?

'True - but - I'm hardly your average stay indoors type - am I? I was always the one going to the parties wasn't I?' You try by way of an escape route.

'True'

'I'll leave it at that.'

Odyssey's soulful notes echo out across the smooching couples – 'and If you're looking for a way out...' Yep, you reckon that you might have just about got away with it by the skin of your teeth. Kudos intact.

'So, *are* you a Virgin?' The words scream 'imposter' at you – in a disco – a Virgin? You are confronted by your massive handicap. Deep breath...will a lie cut it? Did it? No. So... 'Yes'.

'Hah – so am I'. She smiles like you're in that Coke advert again.

'No way'.

'What do you mean – what do you think I am?' You quickly go for the apology.

'I didn't mean it like that.'

'How did you mean it?' Just the edge of that smile again is enough.

'In the - the - attractive way.'

'So, it's attractive for me to be a virgin - but for you it's embarrassing?' Now you're wondering where this is coming from, you've never had conversations like this before with girls/women/ladies – and it's blowing your mind and you're falling even more for this Star Trek-like alien short-haired beauty from another planet.

'I guess that's wrong – yeah I'm all for women's equality so I guess it's embarrassing for all of us – or not – for anyone.'

'You're all such boys.' She turns back to the floor with a drink, but you know the conversation isn't over. You ponder this statement that sounds like a put-down, but at the same time isn't it good to be thought of as a 'Tear away'? Girls *like* those types - well, they did at school.

'How do you mean?'

'Why do you think I asked you to dance this evening?' Now you're getting somewhere, this can only end one way, maybe Malcolm will lend me his car for half an hour? Luckily Sarah doesn't let you finish;

'Because you – '

'Because I fancied you?'   Oh, so not that then.

'Hah.' You try a badly feigned laugh.

'Exactly - we're all adults – a casual invitation doesn't have to mean a date.' I grunt in reply, wondering if that means I get to kiss her.

'That's why I like you Kenneth, not just because we were in the same Geography class - you make me laugh too.'

Strange feeling, something tells you the menfolk are shaking their heads in resignation; but something is also telling you the female species are shaking your hand. The game is up, the whistle has been blown, you throw in a final quip of British sportsmanship;

'Well they say laughter is – '

'– an aphrodisiac?'

'Yeah, that'.

'But why can't boys and girls just be friends?'   You ponder yet another mind-blowing question that seems very easy to answer – yes – because if you're friends you might eventually get to have sex with them.   So, you nod – you hope it looks 'knowingly' then throw in a casual 'ex – actly'.

'Good – I knew you'd understand.'

So – what does this mean between you and me?'

'You – did you – you didn't hear a word of what I just said did you?' You claim that you did, that it was something about being 'friends' but you wanted to make absolutely sure.

'I'm sorry Kenneth - you don't get to lose your virginity'.

Well, she didn't have to actually *say* it – we live in false hope for a whole term hoping to get somewhere – knowing all along it'll *probably* never happen in our heart of hearts, but please don't actually *tell* us – we have nowhere to go when you girls just say 'never'. Keep the hope alive, be friends, let us pretend for whole afternoons of shopping – just to get some clues you tick. You want to tell her some amazing truths – like you don't necessarily want to have sex really, you want to be in love with her, to have her as your girlfriend; if that means sex then so be it, but what you really want is… her – sometimes blokes just want closeness. Phenomenal.

Then she leans in and… once again that brief waft of 'Charlie' before the long, slightly rubbery touch of her lips similar to a Sinclair Spectrum, brush of tiny hairs across her cheek as it runs against yours, nose nudges your own, tongue gyrates inside your mouth but is gone before you get a chance to respond with your own - you have no chance to grab her head or feel her lithe, taught, mystical body, a physical presence that's never, ever meant to come within your orbit this millennia - because you slowly realize that maybe she's driving this thing – is this a demo of what you're missing or is that just nerves and lack of confidence? The tongue, the damn tongue, you knew it. That song should be 'it's in her tongue' It's gone, you feel used... she's withdrawn, you're not sure what happened, you're not sure that's what you wanted at all. The Lamborghini has spat you out and is already roaring away.

'There you go – is that better?' But it's not quite the love scene you wanted.

'What – does that mean?'

'So now you know a French kiss – now you can move on'.

'Shouldn't we tell your ex-boyfriend?' But the look on her face tells you that - once again you've read it wrong.

'What has that got to do with anything?'

'Well – I dunno - he might be angry.'

'Kenneth, you've never even been French-kissed,

have you?'

Well, come on now, when was that supposed to happen? In between making Airfix model kits of Me109s, playing football in the horse's field and listening to Kool and the Gang in Tony's bedroom, when the hell *were* you expected to come across this exotic world of 'French' kissing? Of course you hadn't been French kissed before!   That was more obvious and shaming than not having had a bad attempt at sex. The response came automatically and with the time-honored observation of all eighteen-year old males who don't get near girls very often:

'What? Of course I have!'

'When?'

'Here we go again...loads of times'.

'Well, anyway, I just kissed you because I felt sorry for you – okay?'

You were right. But of course, you go for the opposite - feigned histrionic indignation:

'Huh! – sorry for me?'

'Yes'

'Well I don't think 'Sam' would see it that way.

'Oh, I'll tell him – he won't mind'.

Shit. How does she keep achieving the upper hand?

'You'll tell him?'

'We have no secrets'.

'But can't we just keep this as our little secret?'

'No point, we're completely open with each other'.

All of a sudden Sarah has become a scary married woman who you've been having an affair with and the jealous 260lb husband has just arrived home.

'So, he tells you about people he kisses as well?'

'No - no he's very loyal - and gets insanely jealous of me going out to clubs, but I tell him - it's almost 1980 - us women need to live life too.'

'And he doesn't mind?'

'Says he'll kill anyone who comes near me – but don't worry he's away with the ship – by the time he gets back he'll have forgotten.'

'Ah'.   You allow a pause and pretend to be distracted by the streamers across the bar.

'I just wanted to say that I completely understand that this is just a friendship'.

'Do you really, Kenneth?'

'Oh yes. And I understand completely about the kiss being one of pity - nothing more needs to be said, especially not to your boyfriend.'

Wow, that was a close shave, messing about with other men's women. Last week you were buying glue for the new Churchill tank model you'd been saving up for. This is what they call 'life in the fast lane' you guess; you consider a new haircut and promise to re-start saving up for that motorbike. Hopefully she hasn't spotted your rapid backpedalling;

'Oh, you're great Kenneth, so many men don't have your maturity – or honesty'. A bright, perfect 'D' shaped, teeth-driven smile erupts across her olive skin and you just know her parents wouldn't let you even talk to her. Funny how you've just been intimate but now you're talking like brother and sister. How the bloody hell did you hit the friend zone so quickly?

'That's just me I guess'.

'Now give me a sip of your Pernod – uh – it tastes like Orange juice'.

You shake your head, 'Useless bar-staff.'

Tony turns up and timeless beauty mercilessly fades from view with a friendly peck on the cheek. He asks for an update and you claim the fifth amendment and revel in the mystery.   You refer to a dance and the intimate kiss that you had – which is the truth – and leave him to be the judge.   He asks what sort of kiss, you say French, he asks tongues, you falter, he spots it, you're lost and you're back where you started. Bollocks.

'So you didn't slip the tongue?'

'Not saying.'

'What about Sam?'

'The boyfriend – he's at sea - we agreed she should break it to him.' You're one of the lads all of a sudden.

'You snogged Sarah Craig?'

'What can I say? She snogged me'.

'That's weird.'

'Why's that weird? I'm a great believer in women's rights – why shouldn't they be allowed to make the first move?'

'Because her boyfriend's just arrived.

10: Obstacle Number Six – The Boyfriend

Gary Numan and 'Are Friends Electric' – menacing synthesizer – the dancing stops.

'But she said I was just a friend, it was nothing. Where is he?'

'Over there - and what about the snog?'

'Sympathy snog – nothing - I'm off for a drink upstairs'.

So, you head off for the upstairs bar and try to lose yourself in the largest disco in Southampton with a fresh influx from the dance floor, and yet with a sneaking feeling that you're being hunted and that wherever you go all exits are closed – and it's then you realise that discos are pretty impossible places to escape from without heading out the one and only entrance/exit door and that's going to be where he's probably coming from, like an invisible meteorite heading your way.   A tap on the shoulder – Terry in the familiar bedraggled long hair and off-white suit – for once he isn't the target of some random nutter but he seems earnest about something – and It happens fast:

'Tony's being picked on.'

The last thing on your mind is a pitched battle and gang violence – you're not hanging with the Puerto Ricans in Brooklyn, this is Southampton and you all grew up in suburban estates. But picture, if you will, the average opposition - guy in a jean jacket and feather hair-cut where the hair just hits the shoulders and bobs out over the ears, usually matched with a blue and white (Pompey) or red and white (Southampton) scarf tied round the wrist with a red, beered-up face and probably with a knife. You feel lightweight, insufficiently ready to deal with this sudden menace which will be most likely a broken glass in the face – knife in abdomen – shirt yanked by cage fighter - next thing you know you're being drop kicked out the club with blood all over your trousers, smashed glass all around and an eye missing. That's not what happened. There's far too much time to react – time has slowed down. You still haven't moved. You know you should.

'Really?'

'Yeah – it's gonna' kick-off any moment.'

You find yourself being hurried over to the bar where there isn't the long-haired football supporter you were expecting, but a short haired Navy-type, who is busy prodding the well-dressed chest of a deeply shocked Tony. You're not quite ready for this, the Karate lesson where you swing a roundhouse kick to the left temple doesn't quite seem appropriate right now, if only there were evening classes in sudden nightclub aggression you'd sign up for two years' worth right now. But it's all happening just a little bit too –

- 'What you doing chatting up my woman?'

- the penny drops. This'll be Sarah's boyfriend then. Not at sea clearly. Tony tries to say something but it's pretty obvious what's happening – he's got the wrong person, which, quite obviously and scarily – is you-know-who. Even though you haven't succeeded even slightly with Sarah. But you really don't think you're going to get even the beginning of the explanation out before you lose your teeth, and with a ten-ton piano falling from the sky, your uttering the words 'er I think you mean me' will just about succeed in that piano suddenly heading your way.

'Sorry?'

'You heard'.

Sorry I think – '

'I know your type - students - you move in while we're not looking and grab our women.'

You feel momentarily flattered, but it passes in a micro-second.

'- look I'm sorry if – 'Tony is as uncomfortable as you. But let's face it, he's got more to worry about.

'Oh, yeah all sorry now aren't we - now you've been spotted like.'

And so, this is where you step in – your first punch will go straight to the throat and the Naval squaddie will go down, bent over as he chokes from the blow like Ernest Borgnine in *Bad Day at Black Rock*, then you just walk away...

But that doesn't happen, and as you ponder in your ivory tower long after the event, before you're even able to think about the correct course of action, things tend to move on, with or without you.

'Where you going? I haven't finished talking to you yet – y'know you're *really* annoying me.

'Don't want any trouble so – '

You think you can just wander in and try to nick our women you fuckin' Paki'.

Ah, there it is – and no surprises - the standard angle on anyone not conforming to Anglo-Saxon stereotypes; surely now the bouncers appear, the

clearly defined racist is removed and we all move on.
No.

So, time for a heroic 'Hello what's up?   Your
interjection is a clearly aimed at being a game
changer – but it's ignored as Sailor Sam throws a
punch which connects with Tony's jaw, you hear it
click and the surreal kicks in as the film proceeds to
show Tony being knocked down to the shiny disco
floor, then holds his face in shock as if that will make
the angry man stop – surprise surprise - it doesn't -
and your legs are moving before your head explains
and they're going get the hell out of there.   You try
and shout but it's more like a nervous welcome -
'Hey.' He turns – limbered up and ready for more.

'Oh yeah? And what you gonna do? Come on then!'

A diagonal blur of hair and a Hawaiian shirt flashes in
front of you as things become even more confused
and the Naval rating squaring up to you has suddenly
vanished from sight; in fact he's actually on the floor
in front of you being wrestled to the ground as you
realise Mark has dived in from nowhere like a plucky
heroic Tommy going over the top to certain death.
It's one of the bravest thing you've ever witnessed –
real danger faced with absolute resolution with no
back up, no reinforcements on their way, no Police
force badge being waved, no cavalry.   Where the hell
does that come from?   And now he pays the price as

arms, legs... Mark is now being swung round by his hair as bare fists flail in front of your non-moving form – before the cage fighters appear in their black suits – whilst you are still considering the appropriate block and retaliatory Shotokan kick response, Mark and the red-faced squaddie are picked up by their shirt collars and dragged straight across the shiny, beer-splattered battlefield of no man's land of scattered handbags and kicked out into the cold in a swirl of beer and slippery floor. You remain rooted to the spot. Tony holds his face in confusion. No knives, no glassing, just a few seconds later, and it's happened, and everything you thought was in place – loyalty, bravery, team spirit, you find missing. You know this is going to stick... let's face it, there's no getting away from the fact that – you did - nothing.

Reasoning and rationalisation comes thick and fast, unlike your aggression. You're sorry – it was all too quick. You search for signs of the friendship surviving, but he's concerned with his jaw. If not for Mark there'd have been no-one and you've failed ultimate the test of your friendship, there won't be any others, from here on its adulthood, occasional Christmas cards and long distant reunions. You vow to practise more Karate, think about taking boxing lessons, Judo lessons; but Mark hadn't done any Karate lessons, so what does all this mean? No matter what, this must not be forgotten - this failure. You mention what

Tony could have done with Karate – he says it didn't seem to help you that much, which is a valid point. Looking back - they should run aggression lessons instead.

So, you consider that aggression is more important than any Karate lesson. You ponder where to find aggression. If there are any aggression courses you can start? Will the forces teach me aggression? Like it's a skill to be taught, practised and developed. Of course, you'll learn in time that it's a sometimes-useful by-product of age, frustration and disappointment, but at 18...you don't know that. You realise there will always be people like Mark out there, the quiet heroes who just get on and save the baby, climb the burning building, dive in. Made the leap. The sort of man who went over the top in 1916 and stormed the beaches in 1944. That must never, ever, happen again.

11: Stevie Wonder, a burger and a view.

'An' I ain't gonna stand for It...' belts out from the Blaupunkt whilst the Cortina estate takes us back via the early morning, glistening streets of Portswood, stops at the mystical nocturnal burger van atop the hill where the Fawley Refinery burns the midnight oil from the distant stacks across Southampton water, and the town's lights still promise and beckon to the late night world of romance and possibility; opening out before us like a secret - only we – the Solent City Funkers - have discovered as a reward for our relentless search and voyage of discovery. Strangely united and somehow with common purpose, we shuffle about in our thin lapels pulled across our necks, waiting for our burgers before returning to the warmth and sound of our ride. It's Wednesday morning and you gotta get up in four hours, but it feels all right. Maybe this is how it feels to be grown up, maybe this is what you can expect. Shame it all has to end, because end it soon will.

'Not the best way to finish' you mutter to Tony, who is still nursing his jaw with one hand whilst chewing painfully on the other teeth.

'What you mean?'

'Well – you know – me joining up.

'When's that?'

'Saturday.'

'So when you back?'

'Christmas – I think.'   You sure you're all right?

'I'm okay'.

'Well that's it then.' You sigh with finality; 'our last night at the Top Rank – and we never pulled.'

'You mean *you* didn't!'   We both stare out over the visage of Fawley lighting up the New Forest skyline like some beacon of a potential - a possible future.

'Do you think I'll *ever* meet someone?

'Course you will.'

'I can't dance, can't ask them to dance, still a virgin. It's not looking good.'

'Maybe you should avoid discos.'

'You kidding? I love disco – I love the nightlife. I got ta boogie. it's my only hope.'

'Of what?'

'Sarah Craig.'

'You kiddin'? After tonight?'

'Yeah maybe not. It all seems too soon you know – this Army thing - I'm not sure I want to go.'

Malcolm shouts from the Cortina and starts her up. Tony throws his crust away and makes a move. You persist.

'I mean stay here – as in not join up.'

Tony looks at you, even at 2:30 he looks well-dressed and is capable, even after a punch in the jaw, of being as wise and thoughtful as the Zen master is to Kwai Chung Kane in the 'Kung Fu'.

'Well – I can't really answer that – I mean we're all gonna move on eventually aren't we – it's just The Top Rank – some cheap disco – that's all. To you it's special because – well because you feel you're not going to see any of this ever again.'

'Yeah but – all I need are the BeeGees, a glass of Pernod and Sarah Craig on my arm. I can come back here can't I? I'll have leave, time off, and I'll be straight back here.

'We'll be here' mutters Tony with what sounds like a sense of embarrassment, but all of sudden you're incredibly envious of his situation. He gets to stay here, do these clubs forever, hang with this great crowd of mates, why the hell didn't you think like

this? What's wrong with Portsmouth?
Southampton? The eighties have just started – it's
gonna be great! And then you think back to your
performance on the floor tonight, and realise that
maybe, you, in particular, yes you, need to build your
character, need to get some experience of life
because let's face it, something is missing.

'Do you think we'll remember these nights? When
we're old and sad and with a wife and ten kids?'

'Nope.'

'I will.'

He laughs – 'what - you're telling me that twenty-five
years from now you're gonna be just the same person
going to discos and wanting to hear this music?'

'Yeah – but whatever comes after this just won't be as
good.'

'That's pretty depressing…' Tony gets in, you go
round to the hatch as it's your turn in the boot.

We bundle back in the car and dispense our fellow
disco dancing warriors on their way back via the
exotic reaches of Bitterne, Locks Heath, Fareham and
Stubbington – Malcolm's girlfriend Susie is out at
Portswood – they kiss good night; otherwise it's just
Stevie Wonder telling us he 'Ain't gonna stand for it'
as the orange lights smoothly unroll before us to the

hills of late night Bitterne as Tony dips his head, thinking of the thug you did nothing about. You watch Mark as he checks on Tony, pats him on the shoulder, hops and taps the roof – his trademark 'goodbye' gesture. Mark has got what you're running away to find - to get some balls. The Forces will be your answer.

Soon the Park Gate roundabout looms out of the sea-mist blowing in from Warsash and you're entering suburbia once again. The semi-detached, semi-rural, semi-teenager who has to run away like all the other youths for who the local town wasn't too small but was in fact too much – and be ready to join anything in the hope of finding – what? Stories, confidence, romance... you jump out the back of the boot, tap the roof in hushed appreciation and note the subdued response. You pace up the drive to door, find the key under the flower pot, quietly turn it in the lock and let the damp air and distant motorway roar invade the carpet and silence of the 3am house, where Dad will be up and gone by six. The music is still ringing in your ears, your jersey smells of Player's Number six. Fear. You need to conquer Fear – and Women, Dancing, Thugs. It's a tall order.

Normally late-night entry to the house is a Ninja-style escapade of silent lock entry and stealth creeping akin to Bruce Lee using the side of the foot on the stairs –

but not tonight – tonight you wander up the weed strewn remains of the shingle drive and let yourself in the thinly double glazed metallic door. You want to escape from tonight, but you sleep with half dreams of the club, the cosmopolitan world has been prised open and you have journeyed in like a cultural explorer keen to collect treasures; machete-ing your way through the press of bodies, the sideways glances pushing past, half awake, leopard-skin print dresses and the cat calls of the mating rituals...they're still there in your head as you pad through to the kitchen, spread yourself a peanut butter sandwich then carefully tread upstairs and look one last time from your bedroom window out on the early morning view of the shining dew on the street, before laying your buzzing head down, drift in and out of relived conversations at the bar with Tony, Malcolm and Terry, the fight starts again, this time you somehow get involved but still do nothing, your fists seem to stop in mid-air, you bump into that electric blue dress again, Sarah Craig smiles, purple neon light twists and turns, you drift off again back to half sleep for what seems like ten minutes before – alarm, blink - 6:30. The clock is wrong. How did that happen – 6:55am - really?

You see out the last few days with mixed emotions; one part of you wants to stay, perhaps get a van like Terry, get a house even, like Malcolm will soon. But the other part of you is thinking about bigger dreams, a bigger picture – but it doesn't make much sense right now.

Sunday comes and Dad gives you a lift to the station with your one-way ticket in your hand after you wave goodbye to your Mum from that same weed-strewn shingle drive – you're full of bravado and callously tell them not to expect too much in the way of phone calls… it's understandable – youth – wanting to make a clean sweep if it all and look forward, not back.

You watch the station disappear from the carriage, watch the dream of Sarah become a memory; stylish, cool Tony, heroic Mark, laid back fun loving Terry, confident and stable Malcolm… all lived for the music and the time and they knew how to live in the present. All become distant, then fade to invisible as you wonder where it's all going - then the darkness of the tunnel envelops, you stand clutching your one-way ticket. One-way ticket to the moon – Eruption. Goodbye to the city, goodbye to the nightlife, Pompey, Southampton, New York, Alicia Bridges echoes your thoughts as her voice sings out across those magic hour Manhattan skyscrapers – 'I love the Nightlife – I got to boogie' goodbye to the cheap thin lapel jacket you bought from the Grattan catalogue, goodbye to the eighties and all you had to offer… goodbye to Kelly Monteith and 'Taxi' on Thursday nights. Goodbye to 'Top of the Pops'. Were you going to outgrow it or were you going to find yourself – like Timothy in 'Sorry!' - still living at home at forty? Don't hang around, time to escape while you can, and yet it all feels a little too soon; listen to the heart or the head? The head says go – here is your future – the heart says stay – here is love, friendship, memories. That old footpath down to the Fareham precinct shopping centre – you saw it open in 1975 - that seemed the edge of the known universe – now getting smaller – smaller as the image of your home town fades forever. What will happen to disco? Where will it go? Where will the women go? Why are you doing this? It's for the best, really. You'll come back on leave to visit. You'll change for the better. Won't you?

Part Two: 2005.
Twenty-five years later...

November

12: When the feeling's gone and you can't go on...

Wake up.

Where are you? A screen comes into view, an essay is in front of you, but you can't focus; slowly you are aware of being in an office, you are faintly aware of a presence, next to you – a student – you're at work – shit - school.

'Ah, yes, let me see now...'

'You okay sir?'

You quickly read the blur of print through again and vaguely remember like a distant dream what the essay was about, somehow sum up and make your comments to the patient eighteen-year-old before collecting the photocopying and hurry off to the class, where twenty-five pupils are ready for combat, entertainment and maybe a little bit of education. You'll have laptops ready for those who can't write with a pen, support workers for those who need it, youtube clips to keep them interested, this time you'll win them over. Just, whatever you do, don't get angry.

You enter to a room of resigned faces old before their time, ponder a world that forces teenagers into classrooms during the summer.

You start writing on the board with the magic marker; 'Writing to Persuade'.

Instant groans.   You forge ahead.

'Open the worksheet and read...'

Knock on the door.

'Why are you late?'

'Bus.'

'Open the worksheet and read pages...'

Knock on the door.

'Why are you late?'

'Lost track of time.'

'Right can we all ensure we get the bus on time and keep an eye on –

'Don't blame us we were here on time.' Says the voice.

'I'm not blaming anyone just – can we all just – '

'Yeah whatever' the voice returns to their snapchat.

'Get off the phone.'

'Can't talk to us like that.'

Knock on the door.   You fling it open.

Support worker edges in.

'Sorry – got delayed.'

'So, let's open the worksheet and read pages 1-3.'

'What does 'summary' mean?

'Maybe I should read this for you.'

'Well I just don't stand for it' says the Geography teacher as he sips his coffee and awaits the photocopier to churn out twenty-eight sets of the new seventy-page specification for each student, whilst you wait with a single paper in your hand, mid-lesson.

'I'm in the middle of a lesson, any chance of diving in?'

'You should come and watch my lesson – I just don't stand for it.'

'But you don't teach year 12 re-takes.'

'Anyway - I just don't stand for it – let me tell you what I always do -'

'- thanks.'

'Go on – you're ex-forces – give them some of your forces' discipline! Make them do press-ups! I'm gonna be ages on this photocopier.'

Five thirty and you find yourself ushered into the room with two chairs and an empty desk but for a few pens and a photograph of the children.

'So, we've had reports and we're worried...'

December 31st, 2005

13: The Dawn of the House Party

'Chic are on tour!' You exclaim as you stand in the suburban doorway surrounded by similar couples who've been to similar parties all down the street whilst wearing your favourite cheap green suit with an old Miami Vice pink-striped tie (Debenhams sale 1980) which you've worn for the occasion, and ask for a glass of red but the uncreased, linen-suited Tony says there isn't any and so you say 'no problem' whilst producing your own bottle of decent Hermitage bought for just such a special occasion, Tony quietly informs you that Anna insists on white only - due to the new carpet. You nod and accept the banal clarity of the Blanc, moving awkwardly into a brightly lit, deep pile carpeted living room sparsely populated with couples talking about their children, a large screen TV, Bose speakers playing a distant bass you can hardly hear; you make for the french windows whilst you nibble the Quiche and wonder why no one is reacting to your news about the greatest band that ever lived.

You drink the wine too quickly whilst looking at the LP collection and purposely walk to the kitchen to suggest a Pernod and black to desperately rekindle the old times. You wander back into the lounge sipping the one-time exciting, intoxicating kick of aniseed but It doesn't taste the same as you shake hands with a couple who are looking to upscale if they can get a re-mortgage but it all depends on...

You suddenly remember your surprise – the 12 inch – which you unveil to remind them all of those very good times, expecting rapturous applause and gasps of delight with a crowd carrying you to the record player – if Tony still has one.

'Why d'you wanna bring that?' Laughs Tony with embarrassment.

You wonder what has happened to the world - how did you know he'd marry the girl with the big nose? Why has everyone got a house all of a sudden and why is no one interested in this rare album anymore? You realise these are not really questions, because it's obvious what has happened; however, one question needs a subtle approach to avoid any offence:

'So – you married to Anna?'

'Yes.'

'Why?'

'Because I love her?'

'Yeah but she hates *me* – tell me you've at least still got the deck?'

Tony automatically moves toward the corner and points out the direct drive (less turn-table noise) as you unsheathe the rare vinyl and lay it down with the edge of your palm - at least Tony still has the hardware - there's hope.

'She doesn't 'hate' you – you just said I could do better'.

'- you told her I said that?'

'– she's my wife Kenneth'

'I was your best mate - first – I didn't know you were actually going to marry her'.

'You said she had a big –

'- I know what I said – it's etched in her lack of contact with me - look – I'm sorry, but then she was just some girl in a disco – with a big nose. I couldn't see properly - you know what the lighting was like in Top Rank, one moment you're asking her to dance, next moment you're eyeing up someone else – suddenly you're choosing deep pile carpet and wandering around Ikea.'

'It's not as if we're ganging up on you'.

'No?'

'You just didn't get married'.

'You say it like it was a choice? I wanted - and want - to get married – don't you think I do?

'Not saying you don't'.

'I just want to meet someone I don't have to explain what Top of the Pops was.'

'Laura was a bit young.'

'They're all a 'bit young' nowadays – at least Granny's still going'.

'Well, you're running out of time – they're knocking it down'. You repeat your news about Chic being on tour and wonder at the lack of response - Paris tonight, London tomorrow, Birmingham the next, then back to – you stop mid-sentence –

'- knocking down what'?

'Granny's'. Says Tony with a sense of mock resignation to destiny. You suggest a petition of several thousand signatures (there were two thousand that night when you all sat down to the Gap band).

'We need to get people together – a campaign, a march – we've got to do something.'

'They've all gone Ken, no-one cares anymore'.

'I care!' You wonder what the world is coming to, you feel the youth draining from your stupid pink striped tie – there and then you age and feel like a seventeen-year old more than ever. You take a breath and hold Tony's linen jacketed arm as you fix him with a stare:

'This could be the end of disco Tony'.

'It's 2005 Ken, I think Disco died in the mid-eighties'.

'No it didn't...' you look around at the beige walls.
'...well not for me it didn't.'

'Not for you maybe – but for everyone else.'

'So it's just me then – the single one – by the way where *is* Anna?

'Dropping off Shane at the babysitters'.

'Shane?'

'She's a fan of Westerns – '

'Right'.

Tony lifts the lid of the old Sony, and you remember how you searched through the record stores of London's west end for the rare import before chancing it on ebay for £150 – and as Tony carefully lowers the stylus onto the precious vinyl, the exquisite trombone of Haruko Yamashita drifts out of the Boses and invades the beige hardboard walls of the party with the sound of Friday night once again.

'So, when did *you* last go to a disco?'

'Not the point' you evade. Though you greatly admire Tony's mild-mannered coolness when dealing with most issues, get in a real debate and you know he'll do the thoroughly boring technique of settling on facts, the finer details – thereby wiping the floor with your flippant observations which should never be taken too seriously. So you go for honesty…

'1985.'

'Hah.'

You comeback with one of your analogies; 'It's the same as Snowdon, I haven't been up it for ages but I want to know *that* still exists.

'Well, it's coming down'.

Tony sips his sparkling water as you let it sink in… surely nightclubs were as reliable as Woolworths on the high street? Places that you grew up in, that your children grew up in, that you returned to in order to remind yourself where you'd messed up the first time? In that single, dismissive comment you realise that Disco venues were as transient as the ever-changing skyline of Portsmouth; one moment it was the concrete maze and heroin drug den of the Tricorn shopping centre, the next moment bulldozed into some giant pointless pylon sticking into the sky; the architects waved their dicks around just as much as clubbers on a dancefloor, they just went to different schools and had a stronger sense of entitlement.

A middle-aged balding guy in a fleece wanders up to Tony, his heavily permed companion in tow;trammps

'Hey Tony, got any Roxy Music'?

'Er no, not at the moment'.

'It's okay, I've downloaded it – then we can get rid of this – whatever it is'.

'It's jazz funk' you bark. Tony cuts you a glance.

'Sorry mate – let me explain something about this record...' and you proceed to tell the fleece wearer exactly what he's listening to, that in fact it is one of the rarest of imports back in 1979, that it crossed the boundaries between jazz, disco and Japanese culture; that took several months of searching down back-street record shops before google and eBay were even dreamt of, but he's already backing away and seeking the sanctuary of his matching fleece wearing 'better half', interspersed with other original lines such as 'for my sins' and 'at the end of the day...'

Tony stares at you; 'What you doing? These are my friends'. You motion Tony out to the hallway, through the dimmed lighting, out past the pastel shades of wafting chiffon and low heels.

'One last trip'

'What?'

'To Grannys – before they shut it'

'What for?'

'Because there's more to life than worrying about the carpet'.

'It's a new one'.

'Carpets are for parents. This, (you hold up the Kool and the Gang 'Celebrate' LP cover for effect – the one with the three women standing around looking 'available' in) is our history – dancing, discos, y'know - asking girls to dance.

'You didn't ask any'.

'It's our duty to what John Travolta personified'.

'You're looking for something that isn't there'.

'Think about it Tony, one minute we were grooving to Earth, Wind and Fire, the next moment it's Duran Duran – something went wrong.'

'So?'

'Come on - The BeeGees ruled the world!' As you exclaim this fact from the bottom of the stairs a couple squeeze by, the momentary nod of recognition for Tony becomes one of shock as she hears your statement. Tony motions for you to keep it quieter.

'You say that like it's a good thing.'

'Oh because it was Tony! - and I don't care who knows it – and there was a time when you agreed with me.'

'All we had was a tacky dancefloor and a plastic beaker of Pernod.'

'That's all we needed'.

Tony picks up the album sleeve and glances at the models, he makes that face you've seen many times before – the look of resignation, of acceptance. It'd be okay of he didn't look quite so cool and collected when he says it:

'Look, Ken, I've moved on, I'm just not really interested anymore; I've had a child, bought a house, got married, you name it, done all those things that change the way you see the world'. But you're not hearing him, you shake your head and see the opportunity drifting away…

'We gotta go for one last night – one last effort – I've come all this way.'

Tony looks at you with a pitying, satisfied smile and shrugs.

'I don't need to – just relax – have a drink – I'll introduce you. '

'One last effort - before you lose contact with your roots.'

'Roots – what the hell you talking about?' You're interrupted by Fleece man with a can of Tennants:

'Tony mate - any Smiths?'

'Second shelf.'

You pause in horror, Tony quickly reacts: 'It's my wife's.'

You give the look of the disappointed friend, is this really the Tony you knew back in '79 when the City lights promised so much? Morrissey?

'Come on. One last night.'

'Why – what do I need to prove?' You tell him about the need to remind ourselves what it was like to have a drink, to dance, to listen to loud music, maybe even invite Sarah Craig.

'Why would I need to do that?'

'Because you're getting old – so am I - do I see a bit of a gut forming?'

'There's no gut on me'. You nod 'bollocks' expertly.

'Anyhow, you haven't got her number.'

'The wonders of 'Friends Reunited' It's 2005 mate - gone are the days of leafing through the telephone directory. She's divorced, attractive, and I'm gonna invite her out to New York.'

'Kidding'.

'Two tickets suggest I'm not'. You hold up the expensive bits of card with Virgin stamped all over them – once selling Tubular Bells in a knock up record shop, now owning a fleet of airliners.

How'd you know she'll say yes? Or even be there?'

'You're right - It's a risk...'

Tony gives you the shocked expression saved for sudden meetings with insanity:

'You're nuts'.

'Maybe I am'.

'When?'

You shrug, consider the options, consider your status right now. Single. Unmarried. 45, surrounded by deep pile carpet. 'Tonight'?

'Don't be daft – what with all this?'.

'Why not? There'll always be 'all this'.

Suddenly a rush of air, the back door has opened, you look over Tony's shoulder and see the long hair of Anna – starved to perfection like a razor in a white dress – her eyes dart your way –

'I'll be back in a moment – you can say hello.'

'Yeah well - best be going – buses don't run after midnight – come on – now or never – fair heart never weak maiden won.' But you know the answer.

'What?'

'Something like that'. You make to move, hoping to kick-start Tony into action. You know he has it in him, you've just got to persevere.   Too late, here she is, air kiss, profuse apologies about something, waft of expensive Givenchy, retreat, look of arching eyebrows and sympathetic smile:

'Good to see you Kenneth.'

'I brought the wrong wine.'

'Yes it's a new carpet – but we've plenty of other drinks – how's life after the Navy?'

'Army – difficult.'

'Oh sorry – all the same to me – why difficult?'

'Because I'm in a different world.'

'The real world?'

'It was pretty real.'

She is distracted by a call and her immaculately manicured nails gasp your hand like a company boss before disappearing. That was Anna. Tony knows what you're thinking and carries on:

'Personally, I think it's about time we had a new car park.' Tony has a smile on his face as you both survey the living room as if you were at Granny's bar.

'See you in a year then – it's not me that can't get out'. You head swiftly for the front door and check the time – 1030-ish – shit. You've just walked out of the only company you had tonight. There's something about being 45 and finding yourself alone on New Year's – you expect to be lonely and messed up at 18; but somehow you expect divorce and kids surrounding you by 45, even if it's the local lap dancers - you expect company – of sorts.

Tony asks you what you're doing for New Year's Eve – tonight? All you can think of is your fall-back plan which hasn't been given much thought – a night in with Saturday Night Fever on BBC2 at midnight, with friends it'd be great, on your own it will be depression-inducing suicide.

'You gonna be alright?'

'Yeah – same old.'

'Well… Happy *New* year then…' he says it in that
deliberate parody of American style celebrations.
You tell him how he's disappointing you, how he's
missing out with your usual ironic smile; but really
you mean it, because right now you cannot believe
anyone in their right mind would be turning down the
chance to hang out under the bright neon strip lights
and exotic dancing ladies grouped around their handbags; you know everyone admits we got it right in
1980; so maybe it's not sad to be standing at the bar
surveying all, it'd still be fun, we'd still look good, and
right now neither of us are balding, fat and under the
low, flashing strobes we'd pretty well blend in with
the twenty-something's as they make their usual
testosterone-led mistakes. You know that sounds
creepy, but it's nothing to do with pulling women –
young or old - it's about fitting in.

'John Travolta will be doing the walk in the classic
opening scene – you're missing out mate'. But it
comes out not so much as an attraction but the sad
refuge of a man at sea, waving goodbye to his mates
on an ocean liner as he paddles out into the Atlantic
on a surfboard…

You step out into the bitter water-logged sea breeze
that blows in from the Solent and rains across your ill-
advised awkward green suit that's too big for you, like
a teenager determinedly wearing his best night-out

gear despite the wind and rain because his mates are just about to sweep round the corner in the car – which in this case has long been scrapped and whose one-time occupants are sat around the fire watching Joolz Holland or Andy Stewart – in fact doing exactly what you've just walked away from. You turn with a wave and wonder what the hell is up with you as you make your way along the anonymous streets of the new-build late night suburban estate whilst dialling a cab company - plenty of time to see if the Gosport ferry is doing a special run, then it'll be another taxi to that concrete masterpiece of architecture that is the Tricorn, down the damp alleyway where the shadows move and the homeless junkies stir under wet blankets, before you find your way to the battered door of the lift which looks like something out of a Doctor Who episode - which will once again rumble its way up to reveal the soon to be demolished top floor 'penthouse'. Twenty-six years? Really? Can it still actually be the same? Of course it can, and it will be.

Defiant, you mutter to yourself that it's 'time for a pointless gesture' plus the not-so-startling revelation hits that you have nowhere else to go. As you fight your way with your jacket lapels turned up like Travolta in the last scene as he gets on the tube, you ponder why it is that you have so often found yourself late on New Year's Eve wondering where the party is, wondering why 'it' always seems to be somewhere else, and you decide that it's a matter of perception – if you decide the party is the place to be - others will follow. Maybe it's a confidence thing, maybe a synchronicity of the universe thing, who knows, but tonight you will head for the nightclub, alone; maybe invite Sarah, even at this hour (there's her number staring at you on the phone menu) and at least you can say you tried on New Year's Eve 2005. Never mind the burgeoning self-pity, the childless, unmarried result of too much time spent in the forces. A sea wind blows wet air across your face and freshens the mind, should one stay put or leave when growing up in the Beautiful South? Would I have met the woman of my dreams at the house party? Doubtful. But just like in '79 your ambition took you away from this world – and here you are walking away again into bitter loneliness – out amongst the late-night street lamps – what are you thinking? Well, the night is still young...

You stare at the phone... take a deep breath, look up at the drab Gosport tower blocks one last time and tell yourself the world has to change – before stabbing the numbers and wait before pressing the little phone symbol of no return ... this can only result in refusal, but that's not the point – as long as you asked. If the parachute doesn't open, fine, you die... the important thing is that you jumped. All these daft analogies run through your mind in the seemingly one-hour pause between pressing the symbol and the sound of her actual, real-life phone ringing. There it is. Ringing… Sarah Craig's actual phone actually ringing. Strangely enough it sounds almost the same as every other phone, although slightly softer and more beautiful than normal ringing – you want it to go on ringing forever, quietly invading her world and calling her – showing her you still care after all these years. You imagine disrupted parents putting down the knitting, a father asking who that is and then you remember, she's 45, probably married with kids, though Friends Reunited said nothing. You hang up after six rings. That was enough.

As you stop and ponder a return to the warm suburban comfort of Tony's house-party, a taxi draws up alongside the wet curb where the rain lashes horizontally along the Gosport seafront. It's as if the concrete slipway and iron railing don't know this was the end of a year, that this could be any other night – the rain will mercilessly lash no what matter the occasion; you pull open the passenger door to reveal a man whose weather-beaten face tells you that this is like any other night for him, just busier.

'Ferry'?

He nods, you get in to the temporary comfort, warmth and dryness and envy his calm, stable family life in the photo propped up on the dashboard and ask him to make for the last ferry, past the other younger, wetter, lost souls who've found themselves in the street instead of in front of a warm fire, desperately in search of some form of closure to the year, or the teenagers for whom New Year is just another chance to find a party. All the time the rain washes across the road as nature's statement on the whole event – don't try and give this world structure – there is no structure, no end of year, no Christmas, just this revolving planet; this is your construct, your pretend world of celebration placed on a man-made calendar as Radio four mutters from the radio with the shipping forecast calling the tune for the last time:

'Dogga, variable, occasional sleet, moderate or poor, one thousand and twelve, falling slowly'.

You find yourself muttering to yourself; 'mid-forties, unattached, moderately poor, ageing quickly.' The old fine line between tragedy and comedy… you think how Tony likes to hear about your life but actually living it isn't so hot. Being 'out there' and free without commitments is fine – until times like this – when community is called for, when a gathering occurs, when we take stock of what we are, what we've become.

And what are we? Someone said you're forty-four which is weird because you feel like you're seventeen and then you realise that it's because you're still alone and nothing has really changed. You glance at the warm glow of mid-holiday season semi-detached houses aligned in the street mocking your shiftless bad timing and you think to yourself this has all got to stop one day. One day you'll be in that semi-detached warm glow yourself, sipping your whiskey and pulling a cracker with someone dressed in their Christmas sweater. But it's all looking a little distant right now.

The cab driver punches the worn button and 'Club Classics' bursts out the speakers - the recorded voice of the DJ (he's somewhere far more exciting) announces the theme of tonight – 'a special late-night trip through the last thirty years of music...' and the opening chords of 'Turn the Music Up' erupt from The Player's Association. Emboldened by the saxophone solo you decide to do the unmentionable – flip the phone cover and ring that number staring at you on the menu - okay maybe twenty-five years too late but when again will you have this opportunity to ask out the finest, most attractive girl in school? Yeah, yeah, you know you're not in school *now* – but those days affected the rest of everyone's life. Schooldays *do* matter... a lot. You tried to assign them to the past – maybe the bullying, the humiliation in assembly that time you messed up, the late-night snog at the party and the bewilderment of what on earth to say the next day in front of your friends so you pretend to ignore her, because you're an idiot and fourteen; the suggestion of a date you turned down because you didn't know what to say, or how to react, and she was beautiful. It's all stayed with you. And in our little minds the best-looking girl in our tiny school world becomes the best-looking girl in the *whole* world when we grow up – especially if we haven't seen them for twenty-five years. If you can make contact tonight, perhaps everything will be alright, perhaps you won't care about nightclubs anymore, perhaps you'll have moved on and can treat disco like Tony does – like some washed up relic of the past. Forget romance, nostalgia; that's for seventeen-year-olds. What you now want is reality, stability, a future, a home. Sod it... at least you'll have tried.

The phone rings again - once...twice... here comes the robot answerphone 'leave a message' ...beep...

'Hi Sarah? - it's Kenneth – Ken - remember? From 1979? Happy New Year and all that. Kinda short notice I realise and sorry to bother you and it must be at least 1030 now, but well - I'm going down Granny's tonight – remember Granny's? And thought we could try and get a crowd together and it'd be nice to see you there - and er - well - if you can make it – it's in the Tricorn – where it's always been but you know that – anyway no big deal but it'd be lovely to catch up and dance - like old times. What more could you want – twenty-five years of devotion - now that's love. Hehe – I'm joking - anyway enough of that, hope to see you this evening...' you dab the red phone icon with finality.

'That was bollocks then.'

'All alone on New Year's Eve huh?' Says the taxi driver in a heavy accent.

'Yep, just trying to find where it's at'.

'You not getting any younger – should be married, children, everything by now.'

'Yeah well that's not proving quite so easy – but I appreciate the advice.'

'Ah, no need to get angry. Look at me – I have regular job, wife who loves me, children left home, all back for New Year, I knock off in half hour – bingo!'

You tip the driver for some strange reason, slam the door behind like taking that train from Fareham all those years ago, leaving comfort and predictability for a storm lashed life at sea, tossed by wave and wind; talking of which here's the Gosport Ferry terminal, also lashed by the late December weather and offering a brief, bracing sense of being swept as you cross the un-Mersey-like strip of water – Portsmouth harbour - which is now a churning strip of gloss black liquid you need to cross between Gosport and the Pompey. You decide to ride up top despite the howling sea wind and try to find a remaining clue of romance amidst the moulded plastic seats and slow rocking of the boat. The thumping pistons down below chug away, pushing you towards an 11 O'clock rendezvous with a nightclub, where everyone will be twenty-five years younger and you'll have no means of getting back home to your bedsit - but at least you were trying to do something about it. By now it had become a crusade, a blind test of your resolve; you had ceased to care about New Year's Eve, now it was all about something else; perhaps just finishing the journey, seeing Granny's one last time. Maybe this was why no one got too attached to you, maybe this was why no one stayed to find out about you– because this very ability to dedicate and focus on such seemingly trivial pursuits as the romantic, nostalgic re-visit to one's youth was your failing. Maybe you hadn't lived it sufficiently in the first place; if you'd have got a girl pregnant, shotgun marriage, stayed in town, got sick of the whole plastic world of disco, maybe you wouldn't be doing this.   Maybe. But no-one in that house party were seeing the twinkling lights of the Isle of Wight right now from the deck of a boat – like you were. You romantic fool. You ponder Match.com (again).

A buzz on your trouser leg. What the hell? Hang on, that's a phone. Who could be ringing? Didn't you just? Surely not. You're scared, actually scared. Hurried and delicately you handle the phone like a delicate art treasure to avoid accidentally cancelling the call whilst at the same time needing to answer it before the answerphone kicks in. Check the face – 'Unknown caller' You momentarily ponder the marvel of space age progress that enables such beauty to be brought so close to you through the process of that wonderful, flawless new invention known as Friends Reunited, and your life is about to be changed forever, already the evening is a total success... Sarah Craig is ringing back - you decide on the greeting that suggests you've been successful in New York stocks, flown private jets and now try to feed the world as a spare time project. You're busy but hey, you can make time for Sarah, weren't you at school with me? Twenty-five years ago? Let me think – oh yeah...' That should do it. Apart from the fact you'd rung her first. Hello? Hi? Too formal. You settle on a sure-fire winner:

'Yo Sarah'.

'You're hopeful' says Tony.

A feeling akin to expecting the England football kit for Christmas and getting Tranmere Rovers' away strip.

'What do you want Tony - she might call at any minute'.

'Do you really think I have a gut?'

'What? I dunno – no - maybe it was just the light'.

'You said I had a gut'.

The rain lashes across your face as you turn away from the wind, tread gingerly down the slippery steep metal step and then shelter in the steel-encased chipped paint of the passenger compartment, where the bass profundo of the engine going 'chungga chungga' provides the beat whilst a fellow mistakenly adventurous couple stand huddled against each other, lost in each other's once cosy plan of bar and club. You note a sense of confusion coming from Tony:

'Had a row with Anna.'

'Oh – what like – serious?'

'Yeah, kinda.'

You're not surprised, that self-centred cow, but decide on, 'well I'm sure you'll patch it up'.

'Somebody must have found your bottle of red wine'. Bugger, yes, the red wine, where did you leave that?

'Well look I better go – you're not fat at all – Happy New Year'.

'You left it by the Sofa'.

'Ah...' Think back – you drank about one glass. Good old beige carpet, deep pile...hmm. You imagine Anna's reaction, suddenly you're very glad you're on a ferry, she probably can't cross water.

'Uncorked'.

'Oh'. Confirmed then.

'Now it's all over the carpet.' Why can't it be like seventeen? Mates had girlfriends, then moved on to new ones – you never had to put up with one for too long.

As the ferry docks you're over the hydraulic ramp and walking up the gangplank yet still shouting into a mobile – along with the couple, three girls in fancy dress covered with parkas - all wanting to find the pinnacle of 2005 in this wind-blown sideways rain that gusts in wave-like patterns across the tarmac – you consider summer a better time for New Year and try to remember the plan as you disembark on the coast of the historic, exciting, sometimes violent, naval island known as Portsmouth; like a victorious press-ganged sea salt full of stories of the West Indies and Trafalgar.

'Look – I need to get out – you still on for tonight?'
Tony sounds serious. You're momentarily in shock.

'What? Granny's? You kiddin? I'm almost there.'

'Is Sarah coming?'

'I left a message.'

'She's not then – see you in half an hour.'

You see? Set the plan in motion and people will
follow. Okay then, things are looking up. You jump in
another taxi and head past the dockyard walls and the
ongoing roadworks, down the bedsit land of Queen
street and Alfred street where the locals are already
well ensconced for the night and finally the awkward
concrete anonymity of the now almost abandoned
Tricorn shopping centre. The smashed windows along
the street level say it all, abandoned shop fronts
down Charlotte street confirm your doubts.

'Granny's? That ain't going anymore mate – whole
Tricorn being demolished as of start of December….'

Together you pull up outside and stare - the half-
demolished, concrete jungle of what was the Tricorn
shopping centre, a smashed sign above a battered
wired glass door; dark, threatening concrete avenues
head off into darkness with who knows what down
the end of them, and you stare longingly at a relic
more valuable to you right now than an original Andy

Warhol - the symbol of the time – the iconic black and white image of the profiled woman's head with the spectacles perched on her nose – a parody of the 'Granny' name, as if Granny was in fact a pretty woman pretending to be a Granny; you like the symbolism, it reminds you of Dilys Watling – another TV favourite from a bygone age, you like the delicate perching of spectacles on the nose, and consider that this might be the object of the design – something to do with delicacy, sophistication, masquerade - everything you didn't have back in 1979. It's a classic design better than any soup tin; if Warhol had grown up in Pompey this would be what filled the Museum of Modern Art right now.

Ponder the Icon that is Warhol - if he was to grow up in Pompey; consider that he wouldn't have got anywhere near New York, then ponder how many potential Warhols have been living in Pompey, in fact in small cities all over the UK and not finding their outlet – a bit like you and Tony – Saturday Night Fever happens here just the same – in fact that's a story, made up by Nick Cohn on a Friday afternoon for the New Yorker – based on a local mod in Shepherd's Bush – and maybe we're the same. This is the real Saturday Night Fever – and Tony Manero exists – existed – twenty-five years ago. But right now? The rain slowly seeps down your neck as you stare at what remains of the broken plastic icon. 'Tricorn Shop

Centre' looks down on you from another stained concrete wall, upper windows are smashed and the four floors of a car park Chinese-style concrete pagoda stare down threateningly, as if forbidding you to hang around. You can see why Doctor Who and the Sea Devils chose this location. You sense movement, someone approaching from one of the black alleyways and turn to stride purposefully back to the waiting taxi, half expecting the scuffle of feet as they break into a run to chase you down for the little cash you have. False alarm. Wander twenty yards in the wrong direction and you're fair game... but no – whoever it was drifts back into the concrete maze.

A splash of tyre across a puddle and Tony tentatively exits from another taxi, an expensive Crombie is draped across his shoulders and he stands looking at the remains of our one-time centre of the universe.

'Well that's that' says Tony, neck braced against the sea-born rain with that all too familiar look of 'so that's all folks!'.

'Told ya' calls the taxi driver through the open car window', he's being rained on and there's more fares coming in. 'So, what we doing here?' The radio beeps away, static, rain and boarded up buildings, happy new year.

So that's it. There's only one place left… you open the door of the cab and jump in.

'Hop in Tony'

'Where we going?'

'Where else?'

'No.'

'Millionaires'.

'Too far'

'That's in Southampton!' chimes in the taxi driver.

'I'm paying' says the desperado, which, you quickly realise is you.

Off via the couple of traffic lights and onto the half empty M27 as you frantically text the ghostly, mythical 'Sarah' who has now developed inverted commas because it's like texting a mythical King Arthur - to let her know the new venue, imagining her suddenly handbrake turning the car and setting course in pursuit of your invitation, well you never know. More chance of the actual King Arthur turning up. Optimism, they say, always good. 'She's probably hasn't even heard your voicemail yet' says Tony reassuringly. 'Probably going Kenneth who? Probably purchased a new phone and it was stolen by some fifteen-year-old. Or she has a new phone number, even worse knows it's you and just keeps deleting.'

As the last hour of 2005 approaches you begin to wonder at the desperation. Tony rapidly makes phone calls to Anna who now refuses to hear my name mentioned. So that's two women to avoid in future whilst the meter ticks over and you wonder at your life as the woods you used to play in passes by on the left-hand side of the half-empty motorway.

'There she is, the old Comprehensive' says Tony with a bitter, melancholic edge.

Followed by the infamous frequently flooded 'all weather hockey pitch' up on the hill whose lonely light stantions stand sentinel over the motorway from your old school. This is a fairy tale land of memory – suddenly significant – suddenly lonely – everyone elsewhere having real lives. But now, with families. They are where it's 'at'.

'Now look at us', he jokes, as we sit in search of our pathetic reminder of another time. The odd sad little taxi just like us, desperately searching for remains of the New Year, the hopes of 2006, trying to spot something significant in a man-made, manufactured full stop that offers nothing but two weeks off, it certainly can't be seen on the rain-swept motorway that unpeels before you, even if it is occasionally bathed in the orange glow of neon – the only reminder so far.

So the night becomes a twenty-mile drive on a motorway to Club Classics on the radio and wonder just where you're supposed to be, all three of you, somehow united by your stupid idea and fast draining energy in a last-ditch desperate attempt to avoid loneliness before it's too late, before you're fifty, as the symbols of youth drift past on the tarmac like beacons of possible opportunity – opportunity that you didn't take – the school disco – the Plessey Social Club weekly dance – Air Cadets rather than nights at the pub – so think now and get it right this time.

Orange becomes white, motorway becomes wet streets and traffic lights, directions are given and thin lapels are pulled over thin shirts as you emerge into the rain lashed car park in north Southampton, you tumble out the taxi and slap fifty pounds in the driver's hand, he was hoping for more but the meter said forty, you mutter 'happy new year' and he drives off without as you sense a point of no return. Rain. A queue, and a bouncer. Nothing changes.

14: 'It's hard to bear...'

You sit, trying not to explode...

'And it just seems your work output is unsustainable.'

'It's you that gives me 25 hours of lessons a week.'

'Yes, I know, but recently we've had some concerns about your behaviour being expressed by – concerned colleagues.'

'I may lose my temper in the staff room – not in the lesson.'

'And what with your recent bereavement...'

'I've not mentioned anything about – that.'

'No but, well, we can't really ignore the stress you must be under.'

'But – look – I'm not taking days off sick, I'm not failing at my job – what are you aiming at?

'We think you should take some time off.'

'How long?'

'I dunno – a week?'

'How's that going to help my lessons? Who's going to take them?'

'Well, I'm sure we could get –'

15: Billionaires. Obstacle Number 1. The Bouncer

The first thing you notice is the scar over the left eye, older, but still with that dicky-bow. Same Nazi standing sentinel, still the plastic gazebo that channels you into the entrance and even now there's still the usual group of girls with clear skin, high heels and all with the same blonde big hair-bouffant that makes them look like Paris Hilton. Young or old, rich or poor, you still have to get past the tussled hair youth who clearly thinks he's above all this – who's selling tickets.

'Can we come in?' is what you all want to ask, but that's madness in this sudden realm of attempted cool and teenage posturing. No, it needs the local knowledge to utter 'Just one', or 'yeah membership mate' or some code-word. Tussled youth awaits, judging.

'Er – one please.'

But the youth is suddenly busy and distracted talking to someone else behind him in the office; clearly not the most competent of individuals, all channels filled by this momentary distraction. The bouncer stands at the side, one foot taller and thereby absolved from having to interact with the likes of you. Ordering a room at the Ritz would be easier. Here you must project, force, over-enunciate. You become pushy, your neck sticks out. You remember being eighteen all over.

'Yeah – see you later - what?' A tussled shake of the head. Hierarchy achieved.

'To the disco – can we buy a ticket please?' You feel the eyes of youth beginning to note your use of such a word as a 'disco', as if you might call for the fatted Ox and some 'Mead' to accompany your night's revelry. You hear girls giggling, there's an age gap, but you're committed as if you're climbing a mountain, you're seeing this through. Tussled replies with slightly higher pitch:

'Disco? What – you mean 'Discotheque?'   Just in case the girls couldn't hear. You consider pulling his hair and his body over the desk if it wasn't for the six foot five entity slowly smirking away at your predicament right next to the window.

You take a deep breath... 'Is it open?'

'Bit old for it, aren't you?'

Your worst fears and innermost humiliating nightmares have spoken and become reality; you have no idea how to respond but go for the time-

honoured disbelief followed by class oriented
indignation:

'Beg your pardon?'

'Sorry we're full'. You may not be eighteen, but
experience is on your side, so you go to make a scene.

'But you just let in five people – and you're gonna
turn those behind us away too are you?

Dicky bow and plastic drip feed turns his head very
slightly in your direction at your raised voice. Tussled
hair feels secure with the hulk standing over you. His
face adopts the self- satisfied smile he'll eventually
use when he ends up selling real estate for Fosters in
three years' time – he'll think he's made it then. Out
comes the classic line:

'Sorry - it's members only tonight'

Tony mutters behind you – 'well that's it then', and
you momentarily ponder the fifty quid you've just
spent, but more importantly, you invited Sarah Craig
here tonight, so you're going nowhere. Strength of
character – rage plus age and many instance s of
being pissed off.

You rummage for your battered nylon wallet which
contains a selection of loose change, your old forces
ID and the single maxed out debit card; but it also
might house a sentimental item from twenty-five

years ago, once merely nostalgic, now suddenly imperative, important, vital even.

'It's not worth it'.

'Not worth it? Not worth it? Twenty-five years!

Finally, like an Easter Island statue suddenly coming to life, the bouncer makes his presence felt:

'Then perhaps it's time you moved on'. He flicks his head with a characteristic confidence designed to put you firmly in your place; which is pretty well immaterial because even if you're not 'put in your place' he will soon put you in your place physically so why the flick of the head? Some kind of mock 'I have subtle ways beyond mere physical power? You offer a sneer and small jeer by way of decisive response which has no effect whatsoever but makes you feel better. You resort to indignation as you wrestle with the Velcro of your wallet:

'I'll have you know we're veterans of this disco – do you even know what this place used to be?'

Suddenly the bouncer leans back and places his fingers in his dinner jacket pockets, adopting the air of a shop steward who's fully aware of the management policy he's about to outline to you in infinitesimal detail, before guiding you politely but firmly towards the frozen car park and the nearest taxi back to

Fareham. But you're not going to give him the chance:

'It used to be the home of disco, and you know what disco used to be? Disco was a time when everyone came here - black - white – straight - gay – probably rich and poor - didn't matter - to dance to music you could actually DANCE to - you didn't need coke or ecstasy to get off on it. Kool and the Gang, Chic, Earth Wind and Fire! Nile Rogers ruled the world in '77 and I bet you haven't even heard of him?

The bouncer maintains his stance and you note that he's not much younger than you; he looks down at you both and you notice the scar over his left eye, but the Disco Nazi's not threatening, instead he seems to be now viewing you with a sense of embarrassed pity and sympathetic understanding, his voice is nevertheless the gruff low bass of a championship wrestler as his deep resonance reaches the entire line of waiting teenagers:

'Actually, Nile Rogers started with Chic in 1976 and this place used to be the site of the old football ground before it became Top Rank, and has seen the likes of Jimmy Tarbuck, Ted Ray and Roy Castle perform here, long before it then became a nightclub – disco if you like – which was first called Millionaires, then Billionaires as we know it today, for your information.'

Humiliated, speechless, embarrassed, you rummage in your wallet as someone murmurs about you getting a move on. Tony tuts and wishes you didn't send the taxi away.

'So maybe you better take yourselves somewhere else –?

'Got it!'

Triumphantly, you hold up the Millionaires membership card from 1979. He's intrigued, takes it from your outstretched hand and examines it with a pencil torch as if surveying a rare jewel in his pudgy, boxer's mitts.

'Well I never...' the old Millionaires. Where'd you get this, museum?'

'Let's go – we've embarrassed ourselves enough.' Tony is walking away.

Defeated, you miss the growing smile on the giant's face and ignore the disgruntled stack heels and heroically bare legs of the women as you edge out of the queue, cold breath billowing out like smoke and turning in the direction of the car park - a hopeless middle-aged attempt at New Year 2005/6 as the deep baritone sounds behind you:

'Oi – fellas - get in then'.

An array of hypothermic blonde hair and bare legs looks your way as you march in; the all too familiar bass reaches you before anything else, then the purple lights shining through the curtains before you push them aside and the treble hits and it's like black and white has suddenly become technicolour and the world erupts around you in heels, dresses, fitted shirts, dark gloss, bright colours, rotating strobes and… opportunity? Escape? You're not sure. You have just crossed the Atlantic and are walking into New York City's 2001. You know this scene, and there's the balcony, there's the bar to the left, the wooden dance floor, the rotating stage, you feel the same energy as you head with a sense of professional resolve towards the bar. You may be older but you know how to be confident; keep head down, don't return glances, important people just don't look around to see if others are watching, they feel the eyes and bathe in their interrogative glare. You grab the empty seats – right under the speakers. You'll regret that.

'He was knowledgeable' shouts Tony with a smile; just your luck to have the only bouncer with an encyclopaedic knowledge of disco on the door this night. The music pounds above your ears making thought quite difficult, let alone conversation, short of barking key syllables. Who cares, you're in.

'The speakers'.

'What?'

'Speak-ers'

'What about them?'

'Eh?'

'What. Bout. Them.'

'Are right overhead'.

'I know'. And it's why you can't hear a thing.

'What?'

'She won't be here'.   Makes sign of cutting throat.
You reflect that disco frequenters are probably quite
gifted on the battlefield if ever there is need of a night
assault involving hand signals.

'But you never know, it's our last night' you slowly
mouth the words to remind him. You try to catch the
attention of the minimum wage student – no longer
the cool guy you once idolised in Granny's – but here
she's trying to get her degree - Tony looks around
with a sense of familiarity at a world he'd thought
he'd left behind, but you knew was always there.
Tony shouts in your ear:

'You realise most of these women...'

but just as Tony gets to the end of that line the speakers erupt with the belting faux- Americanised tones of the local mobile disco lad made good up near the stage with a laptop and headphones:

'Big shout out to Sharon who is eighteen today!'

'...weren't even born when we were hanging out in these clubs'. Perfect timing. You couldn't make it up.

'Don't remind me...'

'They weren't even born for five years.' You both survey the scene with a mixture of frustration and mortal fear that you'll be spotted. For some reason Tony, in his thrown-on jacket and chinos, still seems to fit in; some people are made for the nightlife.

'They don't even notice us.'

'I'm not sure I want them to.'

You still don't feel confident; once it was the clothes, now it's the age – always something. What happens to the guy with the slicked back hair? What happened to him? Is he bald, happy and with four kids surrounding him and therefore not in any need of this sad reminder? Or is he secretly jealous of you - you with your loneliness and last-ditch desperation, you who never left the thrill for the compromise of suburban residential semi-detachment. You who joined the forces just so you could come back a 'man'.

The real successes are out there – those who never needed to jump out of or fly planes to make their point, those who had the balls and triumphed on Friday night at the local disco.

'I get worn out just looking at 'em - come on, let's sit in the corner like the old days.' But you've noticed someone, as you always do.

'Someone's giving me the eye.'

'No, they're just staring at you'.

'Give me a chance – we've only just arrived. I'm a different person now – I've been places – gained confidence.' But you know nothing has changed at all.

16: Obstacle Number 2. Asking the Woman of Your Dreams...

So, you stand there in that 'oh so familiar' place; watching, taking it in, immersing yourself in the sound of the 'Trammps' (why two 'm's?) once again as the descending bass heralds the blast of the opening chords and you remember how you once wondered who she would eventually be. But as you can see there's no longer a question mark at the end of that statement. Everyone had their love and yours would be coming – it was just a matter of when. In 1980 it seemed imminent, any moment - a glance of the brunette in the skin-tight neon blue – or was that the album cover tricking you once again? Would it be the friend of a friend, who was it to be? How would it happen? And when it happened, surely it would be trumpets, flags flying, New York and Los Angeles would somehow be involved, and then the usual trappings – house, mortgage, children. But you'd never look back because the future was still happening, there'd be a decent Ford Focus, trips to Ibiza, yeah, you'd get comfortably old because you'd been there, proved your point. You didn't need to think beyond twenty-five because after that it all fell into place, didn't it?

You look out on the dancefloor with the eyes of a forty-something … study the unchanging, predictable spontaneity of three girls who are eternally - suddenly - laughing over something that happened at the bar, something you will never be a part of, the knowing barman wiping the endless glasses who's somehow 'seen it all' and worries about that essay deadline for English tomorrow, the college student's arms full of stacked empty glasses, the pastel shirted, short haired, lonely foursome of teenage males, slicked hair and pressed chinos ready for action, whether it be with a girl or a fight with another guy. Everyone avoids everyone else's eyes, whilst brass handrails, polished floor, the ever-present confetti from the poppers draped over the chairs desperately try to create a sense of party… it was nothing more than an escape. If nothing happened, you could only blame yourself – for here was opportunity. And you never made that leap. The opening bars of 'Street Life' interrupts your thought, Tony turns to you with the familiar Orange Juice. You point to the speakers as if signalling the band is up there.

'Hear that?'

'Yep'.

'It's the same rhythm as the French disco track 'Cordon Bleu' with the same Producer.

'I know.'

'Stix Hooper.'

'Yep.'

'Basically, this guy sees the disco formula and applies it to two completely different tracks – one of which uses an accordion - an accordion? But there you go.'

'I told you that.'

'You sure?'

'Yeah I'm sure.'

'You know I saw the Crusaders play live in Bath – 1994 – small club – like being downtown Detroit when they started up.

'You told me.'

'Streeeet life - shit – is that what we do now – just repeat experiences we already had?'

'All that's left.'

'That's hell – we're in hell – hey - do you think we missed out?

'On what?'

'All this music singing of 'Street Life' – did we miss out on the street life? Shouldn't we be 'burning rubber' and similar shit?'

'You can if you want.'

'I don't even know what it means - 'I played the Street Life' - yeah good on you Randy Crawford, but what about us!' We didn't play no Street Life.'

'We played the *Shi-it* life.' Smirks Tony.

'You said it.'

'I've never been to Boogie Wonderland.'

'Just next door to Neverland isn't?'

'Never felt 'Mighty Real.'

'*What* is written in the Stone? – that's what I'd like to know.'

'Never seen a Disco Inferno.'

'I *wanted* to put on my boogie shoes – but they wouldn't let me' all in all it's been a bit shit really - stuck here in this one-horse town...'

'Never asked anyone to dance.'

'Another drink?

Your eyes pan across the floor and note how this all seems a very small town all of a sudden, the twenty-year-old is lucky that he's got a good mass of blonde hair and his hairdresser girlfriend gives him a special price so he ends up looking like Simon Le Bon, he's got the shirt down at H+M whilst the three laughing peroxide blondes all did a day out shopping at Chelsea Girl and went for glitter, pink or nude high heels, spent two hours on make-up and pre-loaded with a bottle of blue WKD from the local newsagents. The DJ has a day job at the local accountants and the pastel shirts will compare notes back on their merchant ship, before being without female company for another six weeks. Is this Brooklyn circa 1977? Maybe. Like Tony Manero himself sat on the subway heading back home, this lot will be past it at twenty-three, married at twenty-five, just as the college kids finish their drinking and start perusing the London clubs. There's something heroic in waiting and living for the weekend like that, but you can't keep it up for long. Tony edges to a wet spot on the bar further away from the speakers, you casually drop your arm into the puddle and pull up with a soggy sleeve of spilt beer – just like the old times. Tony nods as you regale him with your historical knowledge:

'…then there was Nile Rogers and Bernard Edwards with their Disco formula; they pick on an unknown French singer – Sheila B Devotion and make a hit out of her – 'Spacer' what about five unknown gospel singers? Write a little thing called 'We Are Family'.

'Yep'.

'So by now Bowie and Madonna are into this Nile Rogers' and Bernard Edwards' talent – so they add their magic to 'Like A Virgin', 'Let's Dance',

'Don't forget Diana Ross - Upside Down.'

'Same team.'

'Yep.'

Like two lonely old timers talking about the early days of Hollywood. But as you look around your eyes catch the glance of the forty-something woman you'd normally think so far out of your league you're not usually allowed entrance to the same club... but here she is, long black hair, body of Flo-Jo, style of J-lo in a green dress that says she's out for the night, but she's in charge and yet, somehow, she's lost her way and found herself in Southampton – not talking to anyone - you spot momentary vulnerability in her eyes. What the hell...

'Hey – someone's giving me the eye'.

'She's wondering what the hell we're doing in here'.

'Staring'.

'The black woman? That ain't gonna happen' smiles Tony.

'You reckon?'

'Like you're gonna ask her – she'd eat you alive.'

'Give me a chance, we've only just arrived. I'm older, wiser.'

'Definitely older – the music's too loud.'

'Always was.'

'Flashing lights, everyone shouting.'

'That's atmosphere.'

'You know what?' Tony turns on you; 'A disco is the worst place to meet someone. It's too loud, you can't hear yourself speak, you can't ask someone to dance, so how many distractions do you need to make it just about impossible – so pull this bugger down as well.'

'What about Anna though?'

'What you mean?'

'You met her here'.

'In spite of this place'

'Nevertheless'.

'Beginner's luck'.

You know Tony's thinking and you watch as he scans all the tackiness and loudness of youth and takes in what you're saying. This is a mating ritual, a local Maypole where the lads gather to find their fair maiden, dating back to pagan times, the masks and ritual dances replaced by a new cut of trouser, a trim of nylon, but a mating ritual nevertheless; this is part of a natural process, the fertility dance of the bees, the Attenborough documentary you don't normally see.

'Come on, let's sit in the corner and get ignored like we normally used to.'

With that image, a flash of anger rushes through you.

'Right… that's it.'

'That's what?'

'I'm going in – enough is enough!' You straighten your shirt, down your juice, slam the tumbler down on the bar top.

'No you're not'.

'This is the last night?

'Tis for me.'

 'Then I've got to do it'.

'So, you're going to hide in the toilet again.'

'No… I'm going straight over to her and I'm going to ask her to dance. This is it. I'm 44. It's time. Geronimo.'

'Bet you a fiver she mentions her boyfriend within five minutes.'

'You're on.'

So you take a few deep breaths and place your drink down carefully on the bar to start your run up, the first step towards her and you know she'll realise immediately what's happening and adopt, in an instant, that look you know only too well – the sudden commencement of facing the other way and pretending she's busy doing something else - like seeing an old friend, ordering another cocktail or making to leave; but you put those thoughts away and step out into the music, out from under the speakers and into the no-man's land of the dancefloor – a kill zone for men of every age lacking in confidence – unless you're young and you just laugh it off – unless you're you and you still didn't ask... so you're walking and you're giddy – a touch of vertigo - you wait for her face to notice as you approach and turn but instead she turns towards you and smiles confidently, like an American, like a Puma about to pounce, a smile that an innocent Wildebeest has stupidly wandered into her lair and thought they might make friends. Yes, I'll play with you a while, why not – and then flatten you with one barbed claw of my feline form – a perfect death.

'Hello' she beams with an accent from approximately one million light years away. Her phone goes off – darn. 'Oh, sor-ry'. Sing-song voice. You feel like doing a little dance to it. She cancels it with one long deep red nail.

'No, you carry on – it can wait – shoot'. Caramel voice and total attentiveness with eyes that rip out your soul and hand it back ready cooked.

'It can wait. Shoot' You mull over the words as she fixes you with the eyes of a predatory Leopard. You are thrown off balance and enter the interview room with a fixed grimace and are fully ready to accept the brush off, you understand this has suddenly become a rite of passage; a failed attempt to prepare you for more reasonable offerings. You find yourself repeating her words:

'Woh – shoot'.

'What's up?'

'Nothing – just you said "shoot".'

'Yeah – it means "go ahead"'.

'Of course – yes – right – no of course. Anyway... it's me and my friend's last night in a disco ever, and we – I – just wondered if –

'Vodka and Soda.'

'You will?'

'If that's what you were gonna ask'.

So, you order two and suddenly you don't care how much and you practically throw your card at the suddenly willing bar staff because you immediately feel your legitimacy; you are suddenly 'persona grata' and part of the backdrop to the very LP covers you worshipped by your parent's stereogram on Friday evenings when you'd run out of money. You couldn't be further from that right now. All you can see is a leopard skin scarf, the green dress thrown over the legs that could probably outrun you, a neckline that silhouettes like some Nubian princess when the purple light behind the bar catches her profile.

You think quickly, you note the accent that, just like a saxophone, takes you three thousand miles across the ocean to Studio 54 and dart out your best question ever, born of forty-four years of experience:

'So – are you from here?'

'What do you think?'

'I think not.' You raise your eyebrows in the style of Roger Moore.

'Sharp' she says. You decide to demonstrate your improvisational prowess.

'American?'

'Genius – Los Angeles'.

'Uhuh – I knew it – so what brings you here?'
Seamless, like the slickest there is.

'Boyfriend I guess.'   You're out of fivers.

'Is he here tonight?'

'No'

'You sure?'

'Yes – why?'

'Oh – just a precautionary measure.'

'I see – does it surprise you that a woman might be on
her own in a disco?'

'No – but - why isn't he here?'

'Because I have my own life.'

'Right on – respect'.   As you utter these words you
know they're wrong.

'What?'

'You know – respect for your situation'.   Quick, find
an excuse for that line and run away, but you stay,
rooted to the spot like the headlight bunny.

'Right'.

You might just have got away with it.

'So… what do you think to the joint?' You make a sweeping gesture and glance at the rotating lamps as if for the first time, because it is the first time you've stood chatting to an attractive woman who is clearly far above your punching weight in hair alone.

She shrugs with, you sense, an air of encouragement, rather than an air of dismissal; like a shrug with a sense of 'it's a valid question from a man who I might spend the night with', rather than 'yeah whatever' sort of shrug. You can tell a lot from shrugs when you're watching. You decide to add a bit of flair…

'You think? It's all a bit 'whack' in my view'. Now why did you say that?

'A bit what?'

'It's bad shit – you know – you must have seen better grooves down in New York'. You can't stop this drivel, but somehow it keeps coming. You're nervous, so really, it's to be expected. Total failure, total success, it's all the same because right now you're in the moment, in the groove, in that timeless time-warp that is:

Talking with an Attractive Woman, whereupon time stops.

In the time warp you note thick hair, eyes flashing, but you've been here before and you know the male psyche becomes insanely optimistic, no matter the circumstances. If she's talking in your direction there's a chance. For all you care it could be Sophie Ellis Bextor, Kate Moss or Beyonce Knowles all lined up as the following conversation drifts by in what seems like five seconds or five years, you don't know, because Doctor Who's in the house and you are defying time, Einstein could have conducted experiments with this conversation and changed the laws of physics.

'I guess' she sips her drink and throws her dark hair over her left shoulder in one seamless movement, confirming that she's about ten light years ahead of you. But she's still here, no sudden excuses, no giggles to her mate. Not like you're used to. Now what the hell is she referring to?

'Anyway, I'm so gone from this place.'

'Gone?'

'Solid gone.'

'Will you cut with the jive?'

'Was I jive talkin'?'

She does what you might call a double take. 'Sums it up - okay – it's time for me to go – thanks for the drink.'   She pauses, turns to you, questioningly, 'last night in a disco huh?'

'Yep' Game over. So you let it out with a noticeable finality, for once you sound genuine.

'Why?'

'Everyone got younger.'

'So? These places are timeless'.

'Well, you and I are the only people in here over eighteen. Sorry – I didn't mean – '

'Nope – no sugar coating it – I've done my time in the clubs – and now I end up here.' You watch as she looks around at the forced gaiety and dismisses the dresses the women are wearing in one glance. You decide to escape before she puts you within that lazer-beam of destructive vision.

'Well - I guess I better be heading back to my mate'.

'Is this what you Brits are like?   No conversation unless sex is on the table?'

'But you said you had a boyfriend.'

'So? Am I rendered incapable of conversation as a result?'

'No.'

'You're permanently conversationally disabled until I become single again?'

Your 'no' didn't cut much mustard; so, you add 'Oh come on - I can talk to girls – and women.'

'Then prove it – take a seat – ask me a question.'

You don't know whether to run away from this confrontational Amazon, or consider you've lucked in.

'That isn't leading up to a date.'

Ah.

'Hah!' She spotted your hesitation.

'No – I can do this – so what is it that you do?'

'Boring.'

'Sorry.' Time to move on to your fall-back favourites.

'What you gonna talk about next? House prices and ex-partners?'

So, you wipe that thought out of your mind straight away, which was a shame because it was a brilliant story about how you once bought a flat just before the slump in '87 and consequently had to sell it for LESS than the – yeah maybe not. Okay - stall for time with an improvisational 'what?'

'You were! Man have you got some learning to do.'

'Do you have real palm trees in Los Angeles?'

'What kinda stupid question is that?'

'Just wondered - okay – I've got a question.'

'Dancer'.

'Right – wow – impressive – but where do you dance in Southampton?'

'At the Mayflower theatre.'

'Do they have dance there?'

'Panto – '

'Oh.'

'Yeah - I know – you needn't ask anymore. Long story.'

'Well, it's work.'

'And you - let me guess – two kids and divorce?'

'I know – I look like I should be – but no.'

'Gay?'

'I'm far too badly dressed.'

'Then why aren't you with someone?'

'Oh – don't know - been away a lot with my job and –

'Too shy?'

'What?'

'You missed the boat?'

You're taken aback by this full-frontal frankness of the American – is this straight-talking America right here? You default to honesty, like talking to some bloke since there's clearly no point trying it on with this number – she has you read from top to tail.

Shyness? Maybe. There had been women – all thirteen of them.

'But you asked me for a drink – you're gonna have to talk about yourself.'

'Took me a while to pluck up the nerve'. She flicks her hair back and sips her Vodka before leaning forward with intensity – like setting up a rifle for the kill. This interests her:

'How long?'

'About twenty-five years.'

'Well look (makes a casual gesture showing muscle tone and the intense precision of a dancer – her hands turn upwards and her head adjusts to a precise canted angle) - you've met someone now.'

'You don't count'.   Her pose deflates.

'Well, thank you'

'Oh no – not like that – I mean it's just – you know –

'Because I've got a boyfriend?   You watch as she raises herself up and backs off dismissively, somehow this woman remains engaged despite all probability of having a WWF lawyer as her intended husband.

'Not that this conversation is rendered invalid' (that's not going to work either).

'Yeah yeah'. Sips her Vodka. Looks around at the night, in which a three-hundred-pound pastel shirted shaven headed guy dances frenziedly with a mate in a soaking denim shirt, tinsel hangs from the ceiling, someone sets off a popper – one with streamers. You figure you've had your innings and it's time to cut your losses before you get the big brush off.   What the hell were you thinking? Then again, at least you asked her. Had a chat, it's progress.   The opening notes of Sheila B Devotion and 'Spacer' sound across the orange light. You ponder telling her the song is a Nile Rogers and Bernard Edwards' classic, decide against.

'Look – dammit – sorry – I best get out of here.'

'What's your name?' She calls as you turn.

'Kenneth.'

'Well I'm Charlene and I'm gonna dance'. You're not sure what this means. For a moment, you watch her move like silk sliding over a varnished banister as she effortlessly enters the mass of bodies and is already moving, making the music take you to the Upper East Side and yet here you are – poised – unsure of what is required.

'Nice to meet you' you murmur, but you know she's long gone.

'Well – how'd it go?' Tony appears at your ear.

'I made my move – I made contact.'

'And?'

You look around at the nineteen-year-old bar staff and the cheap streamers hanging from the beams.

'There is no 'and – this place looks very tacky all of a sudden Tony.'

'All of a sudden?'

'Something's changed.'

'Yeah in about 1980.'

'No, more recently – suddenly everyone's so young - we're just watching them now. It's all over for us. Now it's just stories and, worrying about the bloody carpet.'

'Will you shut up about the carpet.'

'It's true.'

'Just because you don't have one.'

'I don't need one.'

'No, you don't need one but you'd like to have one. You're just too mean to buy one.'

Your hackles rise.

'What do I want with those things?   I don't even have a garden.'

'Exactly. You're just envious of what I've got. All that time in the army - your life's been on hold, what you got to show for it?'

You can't believe he's said that – isn't it obvious?

'My record collection of course, when you got married you stopped collecting.'

'You're stuck in a 1980's loop, Ken.'

Tony stares you in the face, holds your eyeline, realises what he's said, shrugs his shoulders knowing he can't take it back. Problem is, you know he's right. Nevertheless:

'Some things are worth remembering.'

'Oh, yeah like Hiroshi Yamashiwa?'

'Yamashita – shita – shita - shita.'

'You said it. You spent a small mortgage on those stupid bloody records and what for? What was the point?'

'They have their worth'. You both pause, you know this isn't the way you normally talk – Tony's had a row and you're dragging him out to this dive when he's supposed to be surrounded by family, friends and a roaring fire with Andy Stewart singing 'Auld Lang Syne'. It's a good point about the record, but then again, if it gets you here it's hardly the best path to have followed, is it? what is the ideal New Year's Eve? Here? In this nightclub? You kidding? You've never felt lonelier.

Tony relents:

'Alright I know what the point was, it just all seems you're desperately searching for something that isn't there, and the sooner you realise that...'

'Anyway – at least I asked someone.'

'So, what did you say to her?'

Waste of time - no one can talk in discos, and this will never be New York. We're about as far away here from John Travolta as we could possibly be.

'Who's talking about New York?' Comes the caramel-lined voice of Charlene, appearing with that super-confident smile.

'Oh – hi - Tony – this is Charlene – she's from - '

'Los Angeles.'

'America!'

'Haven't I seen you somewhere before?'

'Yeah - you mighta seen me in any number of adverts and albums – back in the eighties.'

'Any that we'd know?'

'Albums? Oh - just some disco stuff.'

'Like what?' You and Tony start getting interested all of a sudden and you know where he's going with this... she looks at us like you're two weird geeks at some record convention and thinks back over the last thirty years.

Tony cuts in ill-advisedly 'and now you're in Panto?'

Charlene smiles ironically 'Livin' the Dream, huh?'

'Shit'. Says Tony before he's engaged his brain. The word hits the floor as if the music has stopped.

The eyes fix on you both like a powerful infra-red projector, the words spread out in front of you, slowly, outlining how you can't ever take them back.

'Don't you knock it honey. Livin' the Dream means a whole lotta sacrifice you ain't even gonna understand – not ever'.

You cut in 'Sorry, we weren't - knocking it or anything like that'. But it's too late.

Her head turns slowly, casually, but purposefully… she takes a breath…

'…and just what is it *you* two guys do huh?'

'Well - I'm a sort of - teacher - now.'

'A what?'

'I supply teach.'

'So - not even a real teacher – and what about you?' She fixes Tony with eyes that tear through him. Tony mutters something about his work at the printers.

'Uhuh, right, well while you two been leading your exciting lives I've been out there trying to get somewhere, trying to do something creative, trying to make a mark on the world – you understand me?'

We both nod.

'No I don't think you do…Jackass losers thinking you own the world because you're what? Because you got a regular job but having to hang around cheap one-dime discos like this one to try and get some action?'

Tony ventures that he didn't mean it like that, you nod and throw in a line for good measure:

'Just surprised – that's all – we weren't knocking it'. But she's already withdrawn and is angry at her over-reaction, before long you feel she'll be spitting blood at you. You hope it'll stop but know the damage is coming.

'Think I'm some kinda has-been huh? But look at you - you just a couple of geeks - loser geeks at that.'

Tony suddenly steps in with a 'Hey, do you mind'? But Charlene is ready for him.

'No I don't mind at all. I don't mind that some dudes that can't put one foot in front of the other that can't even dance - are somehow thinking themselves better than me.' You already know exactly where this is going, it is almost like it is destined...

'I *can* dance' says Tony. Here it comes...

'Well he can't' she points dismissively at you.   Yep, there it is. The night is over. Mental breakdown. Depression, gnashing of teeth whilst alone in bed. Roll on 2006.

'How d'you know that?' Your forlorn offer of defence.

'Watching you earlier and man - you can't dance for *shit*.'

Silence. No come back. Because you have none.

You both watch her quickly realise this conversation is at an end, drag her clutch bag from the bar, jump down from the shiny plastic stool and struts off on her silver heels forever.

'She didn't mean it'.

You try to laugh it off, but it doesn't work. You try to change the subject, but it stays there, the truth, prodding you.

'Called 'loser' by a New York dancer.'

'Los Angeles - but what does she know?'

'Well, that's the problem – she *does* know – she's a dancer who was on album covers in the 80s – she couldn't be more the voice of my youth. If anyone bloody well knows it's – Charlene the American dancing album cover queen.'

You look around at the paper streamers, the plastic, one of the revolving lamps has stopped revolving, some cold draught floods in from the open entrance door as people arrive – or are they leaving?

'No - it's important. She's right, I can't even dance properly. It's like I've not moved on from 1980. You said it yourself. I'm still the awkward twat who hasn't learnt a thing – we should never have come here.'

'You've done plenty of other things.'

'Maybe - but in here this is what counts.'

'Only when you're *in* here – means nothing outside.'

'But that's just it - dancing seems like everything when you're in here. It's its own micro-climate, micro-world, micro-fucking-utopia.'

Tony looks you in the eye and his voice changes; 'yeah but Kenneth, there's other things now.'

'Like the carpet'. You couldn't resist it. But Tony's voice sounds over the speakers:

'Carpet, house, garden, patio, wife kids. It's growing up. And this? They're knocking it down Kenneth. Look at the ceiling - it's falling apart. It was just a bit of fun on a Friday night. Nothing more.'

'All that time.'

'It was two years of your life, that's all Ken - look – I gotta get going – Anna's phoned.'

'One last drink?' It comes out as a plead rather than a request.

'Why? Nothing's going to happen Ken. We're just normal guys in a small-town disco. You're – we're - not going to meet anyone or have any amazing experiences in here, it's like you've always lived for something more – but it *didn't* happen and it's not *going* to happen.'

'Maybe not.'

Tony's frustrated now, torn between being a mate in time of need and the very much more pressing need of saving his marriage; 'It's late. You should never have joined up mate, maybe you should have just stayed here in Portsmouth, got it out your system.'

You laugh at the sudden absurdity of it all; all that time running about trying to prove yourself - for nothing.

'Hah'.

'What's funny?'

'Just thought how much time I wasted trying to prove myself – all those assault courses I've done, mountains I've climbed, expeditions to wherever, dormitories shared with other twenty-somethings – all for the single reason that I was just trying to build up the nerve to be able to wander into a downtown disco and ask women to dance. Don't even care whether I get turned down – in fact I expect that – but just the chance to do it – to make that move, take that leap, so that I could look the world in the face and say, yep, fuck it, I tried and drew a blank – hah – what a twat' – all I'm left with is a lingering sense of desperately feeling left out, away from the centre of things. Lost.

'Go on then, one last drink.'

17: Obstacle Number 3. The Drunk Bloke who hasn't got off with anyone

You head for the bar and don't notice the disgruntled, red-faced pressed pastel-shirt that has just bumped into Tony. Short, dyed blonde hair ten years too late; stocky, repressed anger from having not scored again, regulation shiny shoes accompanying the bulk and swagger of an occasional weightlifter who gave it all up for lager.   He'll have his back-up wing-man nearby... and as you try to catch the barman's eye you feel the urge to look over your shoulder - immediately seeing the glistening, red face of the sweating nightmare in the bold blue shirt (the chicks love it); you know the body language; the questioning glance as the eyes weigh up its prey, looking for the opening, making sure he has superior firepower, the chance to sucker punch, it's coming any moment. You've been here before, and here comes panic-time again - slowing things down...

... somehow you're hanging onto the bar and stopping those legs from moving; everything is telling you to flee and put distance between yourself and what's happening five yards away – he will have a knife, there will be a loss of teeth at the least, then certainly beaten to the ground and kicked in the head. But –

no – somehow you stop those useless legs running and by sheer willpower you succeed in gradually making them move towards the enemy – come on lads over the top – into the field of fire, no man's land – and now you're walking into the fray, it is unknown territory, a harsh glare, awaiting the knuckle to the teeth, the flash, the waking up, his little piggy eyes of fury; you see uncertainty and hear his words to Tony:

'... thinking you own the place - who'd you think you are? You need to be taught a few manners you fucking ...'

'Do you mind sir - before you launch into a fully witnessed racial assault – you will be dealing with two of us.' You've no idea where the 'sir' came from.

Pastel shirt is silenced by the madness of your flimsy presence saying such ridiculous words and whilst his brain works out what's happened – then instantaneously assesses size and body weight of his adversary and realises this is a duck shoot – he moves in for the final take down.

'Oh, you're the hero are you? - come on then - want some of this?' He sticks his chest forward as if you might try punching this wall of muscle and bone first.

Adrenaline running, you note the glances and stunned pre-disco fight silence as the bouncer suddenly doesn't exist, the mass of bodies seems to clear an arena in honour of your coming performance and even the glasses and bottles stacked up on the bar implant themselves on your visual memory – possibly as useful weaponry if all goes wrong. The whole becomes sharper, slower, brighter as you take in the stubble, the fleshy face that breathes over you, that heavily, instinctively insists you run the other way, because this is where it starts at 17... this is where you're marked for life.   So, you hold his gaze, await his first move, it's taking all your energy to just stay there and face him whilst he takes you in, sees your weak spot and probably slaps you, which will be enough let's face it. But still, front it out. At least this time...

And his face suddenly changes from hard-lined clenched jaw to eyebrows raised – as a smile and then a grimace crosses his face. He turns away, you think he might be crying but he's laughing, having fully observed you under the lights. You look at Tony – he looks at you - what's going on?

The ironed, pastel shirt holds up his hand in submission. 'Sorry Mister – this is silly – forget it'.

'What?'

'Mate – Mister - you're about the same age as my Dad - it'd be like fighting my old man – forget it – sorry.'

You're not sure whether to be relieved or insulted. Torn between the fight and the chance to be let off – but somehow you don't feel like you've come through this particularly well. 'I'll be the judge of that'. Shit – your blood's up and you've lost your cool – there's no respectable recovery one's you've crossed this line. You stand in the same place, transfixed with the urge to see this through. But the Lynx-smothered pastel shirt has defeated you without lifting a finger.

'Forget it mate - here what you having? - no hard feelings like…'

Tony butts in 'Lager.'

You dart a look of 'turncoat.'

'No don't bother' you sulk, still not sure how to respond, fists clenched.

'You sure?' Says the red face, full of bonhomie all of a sudden.

You look at Tony quizzically –

'Well - he offered.'

'He was just about to flatten the both of us - now he's offering to become bosom pals?'

The Nutter forces his way through the dispersing crowd and heads for the bar. You turn back to Tony and look around at the neon tubes and see the dust collecting on the tops of them, a pink one fizzes then blinks on and off several times – before finally cutting out.

'This is ridiculous. We're too old to even get picked on now'.

The crowd disperse, disappointed.   A large hand envelopes your own, shakes yours and then disappears.

'You okay Kenneth?' No. Of course not, but you try say you're okay – why make it all emotional and serious by asking that? Of course, this has all been somewhat upsetting and a hark-back to that time twenty-five years ago. Distraught, about to burst into tears.

'Yeah – I'm okay, I'm fine.'

'Look I really better be going.'

'You said you were staying for one last drink.'

'She'll be expecting me home for midnight.'

'Okay – so this is it then – our last night.'

'Our last night ever.'

You stare out at the well-cut trousers of what must be an 18-year-old who struts past to join her friends who're all talking about the girl's dress up there on the balcony whilst keeping one eye on the guys on the floor – one of whom is trying to attract the attention of the girl in the dress…

'Never did get the flash cars, did we?'

'Or the flash women. You going to stay?'

'Can I borrow your phone?'

'If you turned your mobile on you wouldn't have to keep checking your answerphone with my mobile.'

'But then I'd know immediately that she hadn't called.'

'Exactly'.

'No – that's not a good thing – whilst I live in hope of not knowing whether she's left a message, I can feel optimistic, I feel inspired – because she might have… she just might have… rung - but a mobile? Just flick it over – light not flashing? She's not called, not interested – confirmed immediately. Back to life, back to reality, back to shit, lack of hope, everyday life.   No thanks.   Right now – there's maybe.'

'Even if there isn't?'

'Maybe is maybe. It's better than nothing.'

You stab the rubber buttons on his Motorola and tap in the code.

'So, don't ring your phone then - because now you'll know for certain that Sarah Craig hasn't rung.'

You tap in the code and the robot voice of doom answers back. You hand back the phone.

'Nothing?'

You ignore him and look out over the wonderful melee for the last time. Yeah it's tacky, aggressive, destined for disappointment, but it's also hard to leave.

'You coming then?'

'Another half hour.'

'What's gonna happen? We're both out of place here. Our lives have moved on - stop hanging around in the eighties.'

'I'm not hanging around. Look - I think I just want to say my own goodbye to this place.'

'Okay then – when you back again?'

'Oh – few months I guess'

'Well – guess I'll see you then.'

'Never did make it.'

'Speak for yourself.'

You watch him move off towards the light – the light of the exit and what's left of the heavy velvet curtain covering the door; outside rain and cold and sodden reality. Inside the micro-utopia – neon, gloss black, the 'nightlife' and that's Alicia Bridges just starting up on the speakers with the thudding bass beat reassuring you –

'Please don't talk about love tonight...'

You and Alicia, together, keeping the faith – 'I want some Act-*ion* – I wan-na live! - Ac*tion* I got so much to give...'

You spin round to the bar maid who is nineteen but might as well be 45 because the likes of her have been working at this bar since you've been coming here.   She's stayed the same age; working in Woolworths at weekends, doing college in the daytime, working the bar at night, studying English Lit' at the local Poly, now the Further Ed' College, probably Photography and Media. Never ageing. The same girl, the same moving on in a year or so, on to college, marriage, children, she's further away than ever before. Light years. You return your eyes to the bar and search for a focus, a task to avoid breaking one of the Golden Rules of Disco:

Never be seen alone for any length of time.

There are others of course; such as walking with purpose at all times, not ever asking for Roxy Music; always having something in your hand, even if it's an empty glass; avoid eye contact with other males at all costs, get rid of all change in your pockets (for dancing or Karate roundhouse kicks) avoid getting stuck in deep and meaningful conversation - and of course - no Robotics. The must-dos are always dancing to anything by The Trammps, Sylvester or Jacko, but never, ever, Rattrap by the Boomtown Rats – mainly because it's impossible.

And here you are, staring out over the floor, alone, failed; beaten by the world of disco you so faithfully love - because it holds its mystique of a never-conquered, distant peak you might glimpse a sighting of through the clouds after a full day's drive. The world moves on around you, and you know this is the place to be if you're nineteen, but it left your station twenty-five years ago.

18: Back at Work.

'Okay Sarah – why did you miss the exam?

'I got the time wrong.'

'Miranda?'

'I was positive it was in the afternoon.'

'Right'.

Back to the interview...

'And your results are down on last year's...

'Two of my students don't even know what time of day it is – turning up for an exam is a bonus. Two students are about 10% of my class.'

'The results are still down.'

'Yes – and there's your reason.'

'Despite that... we feel that compared to the benchmark results around the country yours – are down – and we need to cut back on the department...'

'You're sacking me?'

'No, don't be silly, we can't do that anyway – we checked – no, we think maybe much of your teaching could be functional skills instead of 'A' levels.

'Much of it?'

'Well, all of it – the rest –'

'The rest?'

'Yes there's a shortfall in hours – we'd need to have you utilised for other duties.'

'Such as?'

'There's assistant work we think might also suit you.'

19: '…with no one to love you, you're going nowhere.'

So, you turn once again to the loner's refuge of the bar, to the nineteen-year-old media studies student and remember one probable cul-de-sac you might not yet have explored…

'Do you serve Pernod?'

The barmaid looks straight through you, nothing registers.

'Pernod? It tastes of aniseed? P.E.R.N.O.D. Popular in the eighties?' Never mind.

'Woh' A deep male voice sounds out over to your left; the bass tones undercut the particularly tinny Sharon Redd number playing at that very moment; you can see a well-cut shirt and loose, white jacket, and he's separated himself from two statuesque women that have appeared from nowhere, dressed down in jeans, one with a fur top, one with black leather gloves - ? What is going on – leather gloves and fur in Southampton?

 'Ain't heard that asked for in what, twenty-five years!' Says the cool bass of the speaker, whilst you momentarily pause to consider…

'How did Sharon Redd go from the stunning 'Can You Handle it' to this track in just two years?

'– nowhere near the same thing.'

'and I reckon that's when disco changed.'

'Do we colour our experience of music with the time we're in - or did the music actually change?' Says the dude in the white jacket.

'A bygone era'. You make by way of reply, and with that you fully expect to go your separate ways like the true suburban English gent. But in the style of someone who's grown up without those post-Victorian rules of behaviour held in place, he keeps talking.

'What you drinking?'

'JD if they don't have Pernod'.   The girl behind the bar is suddenly there – and nods and produces Pernod and pours a JD for the dude.

'So this is *the* Nightclub in town huh?' He slowly turns himself to face the floor, still the light silhouettes the figure, he's older than you and you sense a kindred spirit.   You can't quite see him due to a spotlight just behind his head blinding you, added to the fact that conversation between the males in mainstream UK discos is strictly limited to friends you turned up with, anything outside of that except for 'scuse me' is considered confusing, over-friendly and slightly suspicious - unless of course, the dude is American – which he appears to be. Luckily, you're well-travelled and you could do with the outward appearance of having friends so – attempting to strike up a conversation with a random stranger who will probably walk away at a moment's notice doesn't really matter, what the hell... you hand him his neat JD. Fine fingers take it – his two friends glance over in unison, dressed down but still looking very sleek. One with long straight black hair, one with an afro. Heels, yellow sunglasses, headbands, tiny waists, they're already dancing.   How cool, how far way...

'Do they want a drink?'

'Ah no – nice of you - they're always expensive – with a turn of the head to the barmaid he catches her eye: 'A Margarita and a – excuse me - he turns his back momentarily – a sparkling water.'   He turns back to you and drops his sunglasses to throw a momentary glance at you...'

'– dancers – health freaks.'

'Hah – yeah.'

'Hard work.'

'Tell me about it.'

'You too?'

'Er – nope – never got anyway near -not an actual dancer.'

'You never dated a dancer?'

'Or actress, or model, or B list celebrity.'

He pauses for a moment.

'What about 'A' list?

'Well apart from Beyonce – sorry - we're from very different worlds. I can't dance and I've spent the last fifteen years in the forces standing around on parade squares and isolated outposts of her majesty's far flung empire. You? You've got two out there hanging off your lapels!'

'Ah, just friends – colleagues if you like – so she stood you up?'

'I'd at least like to get to the hopeful possible date before being stood up. No – just blew it, that's all.'

'Well, sorry to hear – have another – is that what brings you here? Looking for the perfect woman?' Clicks his fingers - two more appear (- how?)

'Ah, dunno anymore – maybe I'm just trying to get to – you know - where it's at.'

'Where it's at? What the hell does that mean?' The dude sits upright.

'You know, where it's all happening – the centre of things.'

'Centre is where you make it.'

'Easy to say.'

'So – hang on - you're so alone on New Year's Eve you randomly head out to some nightclub – on your own – in the hope of meeting some woman?'

'Hey, anything is better than the usual.'

'And what was that?'

'Standing with a rifle guarding a beach in north Scotland – this is at least a move in the right direction – at least there's humans involved.'

'Hmm – I guess it is - so who's this woman?'

'She's American'. You throw a sideways look and sip the Pernod.

'Then I should be buying you a drink.'

'No – my fault.'

And you both lapse into the time-honoured pause of staring out over the floor as a natural hiatus occurs in the conversation partly due to loss of things to talk about, but mostly due to the banging, percussive beat of Sharon Redd.

'So - what you think of Southampton's finest disco?'

'Looks like it's seen better days.'

'You bet it has – back in '79.'

'But they clearly don't need the clientele – I had trouble getting in.'

'You too?'

'It seems my *shoes* weren't right.'

'How did you persuade the Nazi on the door?'

'Well – here's the thing – a happy coincidence - you hear when 'Good Times' was being played – like half hour ago?'

You nod.

'So, I just told 'em what I always say.'

'What's that?'

'That I wrote it.'

'And he believed you?'

' – he did tonight – doesn't always work – didn't at '54.'

'The Doorman fell for that?'

The music drowns out the rest of his reply and you both resort to the usual 'disco-speak of single syllables and exaggerated hand gestures.

'So - what brings you here?'

'Transport problems – got about an hour to waste – hence me standing here in downtown Southampton – find her and bring her over.'

'Who? The American?'

'Sure.'

'I think that's best avoided.'

'Why?'

'Just feel I'm getting a bit – you know...'

'What?'

'I dunno.'

'What - old?'

'Yeah'. You check to see if the bouncer will turf you for offensive language.

'Who cares? Only you. You can get up there anytime time you like.'

'Not as easy as all that.'

'What?'

'All falling apart a bit –.'

'What – since the Army?'

'Yeah I guess – I had a team there, friends, structure – parade at 8am every day – lights out 11pm – I dunno – things just seemed organised. You come out here and -

'So, you got it all in front of you.'

'I kinda thought it would sort all this out.'

'All of what?'

'Asking women to dance.'

'What – you mean you joined up for that reason?'

'Yep – I guess I did – and other things.'

'Replacing this macho bullshit gladiator ring with another form of macho bullshit called the Armed Forces? You kiddin' me?'

Sometimes strangers can sum up your life after ten minutes – you're not sure whether to be impressed – or depressed.   Naturally you go for immediate defensiveness.

'You can't really sum up fifteen years as 'macho bullshit'.'

'No? What was it then – public relations?'

'I joined for the – for the - you're right - macho bullshit.'

'You said it.'

'– but - different sort of bullshit – different to this'.

You look around at the bar and try to think of what you left behind; all you can think of after fifteen years is not having to salute, losing some good friends in the Gulf, carrying heavy bags, lining up, being part of something – a gang. Guts? Not sure, teamwork? Duty? getting something done despite the world and elements throwing everything at you. Bravery? Yeah, it was there, but a different sort. You come back and - still – the bright lights of a disco – the inability to look cool and wander up to a real, live female – you might as well be eighteen years old - as if all that time and experience counted for nothing. Isn't there a course you can do?

'I guess I thought it'd make a 'man of me' – like I'd come back and be a hit in the nightclub – but what it actually did was just drag me further and further away.'

'Coulda told you that back in '75. Only one thing gonna help you get on the floor and bag more women – but it takes more than Navy SEAL training – takes the dedication of a Ninja.'

'Yeah? What is it?'

He leans in, one of the braids hangs down as he fixes you with the powerful stare of a man who has been there. You lean in with him as if he's about to impart a Great Truth.

'Learn to play the guitar.'

You drop back and actively slump in your seat, defeated.

'I tried – I'm not musical.'

'That don't stop the majority of bands out there.'

'I just collect records.'

'Records?   Dying breed – what you got?'

'Oh, mostly Jazz funk.'

'Like?'.

'Roy Ayers.'

'Cool.

'Manu Dibango'

'All right – I'm impressed – maybe Southampton's not so bad on the music scene after all.'

'Yamashita.'

'You got Haruko Yamashita? Which one?'

'Hunt Upwind.'

'You're kidding – had people looking out for that on eBay – for years.'

'Got it on import – when it came out.'

'Back in 1980? Kiddin' me - wanna sell it?'

'Sorry – 'm a collector.'

Sure - I understand – that's cool.'

Another blast of music, another intro' heralds another escape into the back streets of Detroit with the Crusaders and the opening brass of 'Street Life'; and maybe that's what you like about the disco, it makes you jump from one escapist vision straight to the next. From Sylvester's hi-energy to the dreamy saxophone led back-streets of Detroit. The dude announces:

'Listen man, you ain't gonna meet your wife out there, not when you can't even hear her speak!'

You've known this for some time.

'I know – but I just wanna be like it was at eighteen, you know - there was a future, hope, we had time.'

'Oh, there's still time.'

'I think I've had mine. Look what's happened to the music - remember the days of 'Chic'? Jazz Funk? We all thought that Disco was forever – we didn't realise it was gonna die away and end up with DJs playing the shit they do now – snippits of Jackson, snippits of Earth, Wind and Fire.

He nods, you look around at the peeling paint.

'Bernard Edwards, Tony Thompson.'

'What you say?'

'Two names that just drifted past in the night – Chic's drummer and – '

'Yeah I know… no one notices huh?'

'Well – you might see it on some websites but - it should be all over the place – and what's more they're pulling this place down.'

The 'dude' – for that is what he exudes and what he has become – leans in and gestures with a sweep of his drink, and you think you might have seen him before.

'Listen – you can't be much younger than me - you remember back in '79? They had a mass burning of disco records. Disco officially sucked.'

'That's when we were just about getting into it here.'

'Been and gone by then – but my friend, did Disco die?'

'No!'

'Exactly.'

'But what about Studio 54?'

'Studio?'

'Wasn't that shut down in '81? *The* home of disco?'

'Yeah – and they wouldn't let us in.'

'You? You were there?'

'One time – just the once.'

'Shoe policy again?'

'Always the shoes – we went back and wrote a song about it.'

'Hah – you get a number one hit?'

'It did alright – look I better be going - small word of advice - I'm sensing you want a woman because you don't want to feel alone – that it?'

The sax solo of Wilton Felder invades the moment. You both pause to listen and hear it echoing out the bar across the orange-lit Detroit street.

'You think that's the answer, don't you?'

What's he talking about?

'And you don't?'

A beautiful woman is always the answer.

'No I don't. You can be in the middle of a marriage, living the high life, travelling around the world constantly - and feel like the loneliest dude on the planet.'

'Bowie said it - 'I'm the luckiest man in the world - not the loneliest' but it was if he was saying it to reassure himself in the song.'

'Exactly. Why do you think I wander in here on New Year's Eve?'

'I dunno – you're not lonely' you point at the accompanying ladies now grooving it up on the floor. Man, they look good.

He shrugs. 'Maybe not – I guess.'

Suddenly Disco Nazi appears at the dude's shoulder like an obsequious servant and looks with what can only be considered 'wonder' at you and the dude having a chat.

'Excuse me sir – the vehicles been fixed and it appears they are ready to go.'

The dude waves at the ladies and they're coming over. He addresses you square on. You begin to put and two and two together... dreads, accent, then you start drifting into shock, but before you can, it's as if he sees it dawning on you and so he's up and going before turning back one last time and fixing you with a raised eyebrow…

'They're still playing our records and I'm *older* than you, I wasn't *allowed* in to Studio - and when disco officially *sucked* I didn't fit *in*. Did I care? Did I let that stop me? And I *wrote* the darn music! So, stop giving yourself excuses… anyway, better go. Nice meeting you Kenneth – this is a new year – this is the one.'

'You too Mister -' with that he slipped down from the stool, held out his hand to shake and shook your hand with both of his own – someone had appeared at the door – gave them a wave and disappeared towards the flickering light of the beckoning January. The air momentarily blows in like the door like it's been thrown open by a storm, then closes in on the fantasy land once again. Suddenly the walls are even more paper thin than before, the barman looks like he will drop out of college, move back in with his Mum, the party poppers are from the pound store, the owner is using his Dad's money, the tinsel wallpaper is scratched off in places. Only the records are real.

'Was that who I think it was?' comes the voice from nowhere, until you realise it's the Nazi, with a look of sudden respect for you.

'Who do you think it was?'

'Hmm – it was - wasn't it?'

'Might have been…'

'Didn't introduce us?' You turn and there's Charlene at your shoulder completing the confusion.

'Nope - sorry.'

'Why was he talking to you?'

You do your best attempt at shrugging it all off as 'a long story', which seems to work as you try to regain what the hell had just happened.

'So – while I'm here – you wanna drink?'

She moves her hand and by magic the barman reads her mind and starts the process. To add to the mayhem a woman has just strutted in through the door in gold heels and loose one-piece black trouser suit and lit up the surrounding floor. What do they say about buses? Her familiar jawline profiles against the misty smoke machine mingled with the backlight – making her look as if she's something out a New Romantic Music Video – 'Vienna? – Rio?'. Yeah that's it. She launched a thousand fantasies back in school – and this glimpse of her profile reminds you why like an aching pain.

'Shit – it's Sarah Craig.'

Charlene follows your eyeline. 'Who's that? The love of your life?'

'I was at school with her – many years ago.'

'That it?'

'We go back a long way.'

'Oh, another one?' Mumbles the Nazi, still hanging about.

'From school.'

'Really – where'd you go – Hollywood high?'

Charlene seats herself at the bar and sips her Manhattan that has appeared in the blink of an eye.

'Okay – shall I stay or do you wanna introduce me?'

Charlene raises her eyebrows, the disco Nazi seems to consider himself part of the conversation, Sarah Craig floats through the throng like Alicia Bridges on the cover of her album with short, jet black hair and silk, platforms, triangle smile. You've just jumped aboard a private jet and crossed an ocean.

Then Charlene clicks her fingers and fixes you with a look that would bewilder a Cobra in mid strike:

'You were at school with her - that's all. Doesn't mean you're in love with her. Just nostalgia kicking in.'

You would like to take that all in but Sarah has already spotted you and started towards you as a golden path lights her way and somehow you remember why she's here – that she must have got your call – and is coming to see *you* – suddenly her eyes and smile and teeth are on you and you might as well have just bought a Porsche 911 with Quincy Jones playing in the back and had your exclusive invite to the Oscars come through the door - all at once – here she comes – arms loose – thin gold belt – olive skin – men look over their shoulder – then look at you – and the path opens like the crowds in the Tour De France as the cyclists approach the summit of the Col and you wonder as to what special buttons you pressed, what formula you used to achieve such unwarranted success as this right now; is there an algorithm you need to commit to memory? A self-help book? Her feet carry her as if on a magic carpet, time is standing still. It truly is New Year's Eve – right now. Black hair, teeth, heels, blue eyes catch the light - Yes - you are now 'The Dude'.

Her smile explodes in the space between you:

'Hi Kenneth.'

'Sarah – I don't believe it.'

'Maybe not then' Charlene mutters. But Sarah's strong Hampshire accent cuts through the speakers in deep contrast to the American twang:

'Thought I'd see how you were. Sorry - I got caught at another party.'

You stumble out the words 'Sarah – how are you? – All these years – must be twenty-five – you look great though.'

'I'm good. Still doing the Discos then?'

'No, this is the last night.' She averts her eyes and her organic lasers stop burrowing into your skull.

'Let me just text John to let him know I'm here.'

And up comes the dreaded opening chords of 'Three Times a Lady', Sarah is now in front of you and you note her lithe, trained arms and the way her hair falls straight and in front of her face. Great, just you two together looking like extras from Miami Vice. A guy in a white suit asks what you're drinking – you say single malt – he orders two and slides one down – you wave a 'cheers' and he does that gesture where he just points at you – international language for 'you're the man' as he notes you're being approached by women of Sarah's calibre. You're there. In the Club, ruling. The Dude – where it's at.

'Is he the jealous sort?'

'John? – no - if only.'

'I only ask – after – y'know…'

'What?'

'Last time.'

'Why? Oh - what Sam? (she laughs) wasn't that funny?'

'Ha yes - well – I mean - not really – not for Tony.'

No of course not; Sam was far too insecure - that's why I left him – anyway never mind that – hasn't changed much has it?'

'Not much – so John's The One is he?'

The one-time icon that was – is – Sarah, looks around the club like a newly crowned Queen surveying her kingdom. Her olive-skinned jaw juts from under her hair, still cut short like it used to be in the late 70s, before anyone had written about Ferris Bueller or the Breakfast Club, before you knew how to deal with impossibly attractive girls that needed nothing more than socially connected friends. When she turns to speak to you her close-set eyes almost cross – and yet somehow that makes her more beautiful than ever and you remember how she looked at you when you gave her a lift on the bicycle back in '76 – when she wore the grey and white pinstripe dungarees whilst sitting on your saddle, you on the crossbar and all the other 14 year olds wishing they were you. But never beyond that – asking you to sit further away when the long-awaited fifteen-year-old Christmas party came around - because they might think she was with you... so you got drunk on cider, then kissed by some girl with a boyfriend out of pity and cycled home in time for Parkinson's interview with Twiggy on BBC1, which you sat and watched in front of your parents as if you weren't in the least bit drunk. Classic 70s experience in retrospect. Clearly something memorable had happened, but it wasn't quite what you wanted. Funny how that became a microcosm for your life.

'Well he'll do - know what I mean? Security an' all that - you know how it is.' Harsh.

Lionel Ritchie adds with sincerity '...and thanks, for the times, that you've gi-ven me, the memories are all - in my mind...'

'Fancy a slow dance?' All you can think of is why now? Why not back in '79? Sarah is asking you to dance and you're suddenly aware that Charlene has disappeared from the table, so has the bouncer.

'Love to – but' – you look around, realise that she's gone - the pissed off, washed up ex-dancer with a dose of New York/LA attitude.

'Look, I'm really sorry, normally I would, but I gotta go and speak to someone'.

'Really? Used to be a time when you'd drop anything for a dance with me.'

'Yeah, true, I know – but – sorry – gimme a moment.'

'You want a moment?'

You've just walked away from someone you would kill all your life to be with – all because you want to find someone you just met – you scan the bar and then race up the stairs, she was as pissed off as you about the way life worked out; she was washed up on the shore of a disco in her forties – just like you. True – she could dance and you couldn't – had weathered better than you. But other than that, you were strangely similar in outlook as you see her heading for the door with her coat - for once somebody who – despite the ability to wear leopard skin and heels – likes talking to you. You never knew such women.

'Charlene – can I speak?'

'I don't know – can you?'

'I didn't mean to offend - I was just surprised to see her that's all.'

'What do I care - good luck.'

'Do you wanna – you know?'

She looks at you and makes lightning calculations far outside your speed of logic. Her jaw juts sideways and her left shoulder drops to allow her to look at you in the manner of someone weighing you up as worthy of her time. It could go either way…

She starts dancing effortlessly as if you're not there and with that true freedom you never understood, like she was born to this whilst making the 'safe' couples suddenly look a little too conventional, a little too south coast, a little too English… you see her as that woman you've seen many times before… and that's when you note a gesture she does right there – a flick of the skirt- a glance – a throw of the hair. Perhaps it's the light that silhouettes her like some 1920s art-deco sculpture, timeless, not of this place. Perhaps it's something more than that. You're not sure, but something rings a bell… The Player's Association belts out for the second time that night.

'Sorry? I can't hear you – what you trying to say?'

'Just wondered if…'

'You're too quiet – you'll have to speak up.'

Her hostility gets to you, sends out that sign you've known before and remembered the lesson learned from ten years ago when you took the opinion that someone could be convinced to try you out – bad idea.

'Nothing. Sorry'. You retreat into the half light of the slow dance light show, which consists of a few violets and yellows that float aimlessly across the floor.

You're lost in the sudden attention from two angles, which is the story of your life; you're very good at coping with one visitor at a time, friends you left behind from the forces, normally you face the drought with a sigh of resignation and plod your Sundays to a seat in the cinema, getting used to the lack of arguments over what to watch, and now this.

'Something about dancing?'

 'Yes – if you wanted to dance.'

'Oh – you're asking *me* to dance?'

'Yes.'

'Okay.'   There must be something wrong, there must be something – some reason this man-eating icon of disco has accepted you when so many have turned their noses up before you even get near. But then she puts her hand on her hip and fixes you with a look that drills right through you.

'Thought you didn't.'

'I don't. But - I'll try. Even if you do have a boyfriend.'

'I don't.'

'But - you said -'

'Guys don't like it when I keep saying 'no'. Anyway - since you asked.'

She starts moving – you hold her like you're handling a 3000-year-old Ming dynasty vase when it should be like a female Jaguar on the loose, so you give up and go for the ass and pull her towards you expecting the requisite slapped face, she immediately fits your contours and it feels like a jigsaw is suddenly complete.

'Now you're learning.'

'Taken twenty-five years.'

The distorted microphone of the DJ pipes up; 'Okay everyone get ready - in ten nine - eight - seven - six - five four - three - two - one - Happy New Year everyone - Happy New Year.'

'Make that twenty-six' she shouts in your ear but it still feels sensuous. The opening chords of the Bee Gees and you're off.

'You're right - you are bad.'

'Told you.'

'You just need to relax more. Try bending your knees.'

'Here we go.'

'Hey by the way - that band I did the cover for – '

'Go on.'

'It was something like 'Turn the Music Up'

'You're kidding, by The Players Association?'

'You know it?'

You run over to the wall and point at the cover – she stands bemused. She adopts that look that says she remembers this shot all too well, yet doesn't in any way want to go back there, back to the lithe golden body dressed in gold silk, with that good time girl look she pulled off so well, and thereby revealing the fundamental difference between men and women. Nostalgia, she doesn't need it. Her voice reveals a thousand mixed memories:

'That's the one, they played it over the speakers. Must have jogged my memory.'

'You're the girl from the cover - you *are* Disco.'

'I am?'

'I've known you for twenty-five years. As long as Sarah Craig, maybe longer.'

'Think you're in love with the wrong thing – where she go?'

'Oh - I think I might've offended her.'

'So - what you gonna do now?'

'What do you mean?'

'This disco is closing – you're getting older - where you gonna go now?'

'I've got tickets to New York – wanna come?'

Part Three: 2016.

Another eleven years on.

20: Back in class

'Dominic, put the phone away.'

'Nope.'

'Put the phone away now.'

Starts texting.

'In which case get out of my class - now.'

'Fuck you - I'll take my time thank you very much.'

'I presume I can quote you on that – get out – now.'

'You can go fuck yourself for all I care.'

'Get out of my class before I – before I lay one on you.'

'I presume I can quote *you*…'

21: 'Lately…'

You don't go to Discos now. No one does really. DJ's
never play the whole record - they just drift one
amorphous track into the next – and thereby destroys
the whole identity of the single. You just listen to
Alicia Bridges on your smartphone Spotify App. You
Facebook Tony and ask him what he's doing for
Christmas. Well, you know what he's doing – he'll be
with the family – you've seen the photographs and
'liked' the image of the Christmas meal she'd served
up with the servant's help – sorry – 'housemaid'. No
one's going to Discos now. Why would they? They
got bulldozed. Now they meet on Grinder or Tinder
or chat via Kik or Snapchat or Instagram or Watzap
but still have trouble replying or getting them when
you want them, because there's no need to see each
other. Apparently the 17 year olds have retaliated
with an ironic retro revival attack on the dancefloor –
but that's all it is – ironic. Like the comedy, the music;
the excuse for not trying very hard. Bitter? Yes.
Lonelier than ever? Yes. Irony? Nope.

But you'll see her tonight at least.

You know you could just get out there on your own
and march in past the bouncer, pay your money and

stand about at the bar like some regular who's not aware they've transformed the old pub into a nightclub. But 'nightclub?' Do they still have them? You see the streets behind Southampton's London Road and there's still women in gloss platform heels like there's always been since 1980. You wander past the same old queue, daring not to look for being accused of letching, but their same bare legs provide a flash of white and pink contrasting with their same paper thin spangly black nylon things they've thrown over their same freezing torsos as they totter and flirt with the same old bouncer inside the same old gold rope that separates them from the same old 'other world' of empty glitter indoors that you fell for – like an idiot.

So now you meet in restaurants – the places you avoided when 17 because it was people sat around – talking.

You're first there, in the restaurant down by the boat yard in Bursledon where you feel like you should own a yacht because there's so many of them outside bobbing about and what with the wooden beams and paintings of yachts, you're mildly surprised to find it fully booked with non-owning yacht families all photographing their meals of battered fish. You only used to look at this brightly lit place across the harbour on the way to the Top Rank; now you're here it feels disappointing; like just another haven for married couples. So, you sit, sipping your orange juice looking across to the boat-yard where the rich buy their yachts and organise full-blown family meals where the son and his dutiful, pretty new girlfriend sit on the end table and discuss plans. You remember those days, you even remember her.

'You're looking smart' nods Tony as he appears from nowhere and silently sits down. He looks younger than you, effortlessly dressed in linen jacket and Italian shirt; you know better than to try this approach to fashion.

'Look at you.'

'Well, Sarah's coming isn't she.'

You order the whitebait, he the starter, nothing more. No alcohol. Once again, you find yourself removed from the normal course of events, maybe that's why you know him.

'I just expected to have kids, a wife, but Charlene didn't want it – and I'm not going to start looking around for some kind of baby donor, if it's Charlene, then it's Charlene I stay with – with or without children.'

Tony sips his juice.

'But she won't live with you?'

'Nope – ain't gonna happen, I guess I made a bad choice – I dunno – we read each other's thoughts and... maybe I did leave this place too soon – maybe the forces – maybe ambition – was all a mistake, just like that flat I bought that lost eleven grand. So I'm left hanging around outside or in the corner of bars at this time of year trying to find out where I'm supposed to be.'

'But that's the sort of person you are – always looking ahead, go-getting.'

'– but you know where I'm gonna be come New Year's Eve? '

'Trafalgar Square?'

'A hotel in Southampton.'

'Why there?'

'I've invited her down. She may come, she's staying with a friend in London for the week. Main thing is if she doesn't then I can guarantee a good time. On my own if I have to. What about you?'

'We'll just get a small place somewhere – together.'

You check your phone – Sarah 'I can't escape... say hi to Tony and we'll meet up soon x.'

Unsurprised you finish the small meal, shake hands, pat each other on the back and set out in separate cars back to your very separate lives. Tony to a world of a caring wife, an extended family and a house by the sea.   You to a hotel.

Yeah, that's you, ambitious, go getting, trying to do something; you've got friends who are go-getting, ambitious, and yet they're also spending New Year with their wives, husbands, girlfriends and casual affairs. Ambition is not your excuse anymore.

OkCupid yields the usual array of wealthy ex-wives with grown up children who regard a glass of 'vino' as a fitting reward for their day at the office, Guardian Soulmates offers their own houseboat and cycle rides, and you wonder if Tinder would yield more success in terms of someone not settling in for death. Is it going to be the same next year – and the next? Is this the way it is now?

You wake up in your Dad's bungalow amidst the thrown across sheets and half-made bed. The text pings.

Charlene: She's sorry – couldn't get away. Turns out she couldn't even make it onto the plane.

You stand looking in the window of the Army Careers' Office and note how it's changed from its original premises a few doors down the street; now it advertisers all the protection and body armour worn by soldiers, as if comically advertising how well protected you are if you're going to be volunteering to be a target for a few years, but no protection from the psychological stress of being torn away from what was the Early Days of Disco – from all you knew - and then coming back to an empty shell. You note that the stairway down to the room where you swore the oath has gone – maybe it wasn't real – nor was the oath - just a fantasy at the time – as was the Russian threat. It was here you signed up in 1981 and your adventure began, here that disco stopped, Steve Rubell of Studio 54 would have commiserated with you as he lay dying of Aids. It was here that things changed forever.   You finish your Subway and throw the remains in the overflowing bin, the Bargate centre has closed, all down the street shops are boarded up, just like the 1970s. The homeless nestle under lampposts outside Superdrug, relegated from Tesco. You feel you have too much in common - so you drop fifty pence into the cap and reassure yourself with the distance again.

Plan B. The day timidly drifts into evening and the dreaded New Year's Eve beckons like an empty conch shell stranded by the tide. You check in to the Grand Harbour Hotel amidst Japanese couples who thought it might be a good idea, the odd mistaken European group and anyone else who thought a night in a hotel a 'nice change' before realising they were in a forgotten seaport in winter – because Britain celebrates New Year by the fireside.

You get a taxi to London road, find 'Street Level' once again – now the Sadler's Brewhouse - it's turned into a 'gastro bar' where families gaze around wide-eyed and Mum buys Steak for the teenagers who'd rather be with their mates. The rest have just decided this is where they'll be and booked tables - which is similar to what they've done with their lives. Or maybe they booked just in time, it's you that's left it too late. They went for community, you for ambition – the record is stuck.

Over to another bar where it's now a five-pound entry fee – girls in white floaty dresses inside suggest some form of life, but you're not paying to enter a pub and so get a taxi back to the Juniper Berry on the City wall, where there's someone with a guitar, the requisite sixteen year-old followers in heels and massive drawn-on eyebrows hanging around; you're not sure who is the performer and who's the spectator, as the 17-year-old guitarist doesn't really care what he plays - the important thing is having a guitar, a checked shirt, a cap and a sense of being above all else in that bar. You don't really blame him. You feel outside, like being posted to an Army camp back in '82 here you wandered the streets of St Andrews and looked in the windows at the groups of students all animated in their conversations about – something – something you were not a part of part – thirty-five years later and you're still not a part of it.

As you duck between alleyways you come upon tented areas fenced off where geezers employed as bouncers await punters with pumping bass and empty space. It's all a bit pathetic. But it'll liven up. You're not going to wait, and anyway, you're thirty-five years too late.

The taxi driver sums it up with a philosophical overview 'it all changed in 2000, when the bars started charging and the clubs made it £30 entry. So, everyone buys from supermarkets to pre-load and don't head out 'til 10-11 o'clock – couldn't do that in 1980 – no need. It used to be full of people at 8.' You agree, you remember. You were there.

Back into the Grand Harbour hotel bar and it's populated by a bag-pipe player awaiting his gig, a lone woman reading the paper and about three couples who find you standing alone in the middle of the room far more interesting than their conversation that petered out half an hour ago. They'll spend the rest of the evening checking their watches and realising that this isn't where it's at.

You sip your wine at a table with the dregs of a party who have long since departed for where it actually is 'at'. And you ponder why, oh why, you find yourself so high and dry on this night every year.

Was it because of that night in 1979? Did that set your expectations too high? Granny's Discotheque nightspot - your escape from the home, your entrance into adulthood; did you think that with money and maturity you'd locate where it's at and stay there? Like your disco friends, Mark, Terry and Tony – who all got families. One soulmate encounter and you're cured of this.

Ping goes the text...

Charlene: 'Did you hit the clubs?'

'No.'

What's that supposed to mean? A question? Means nothing. Disco only exists on Heart FM Club Classics.

You lay on the bed and watch TV, fall asleep and wake up to Dragon's Den – the chip shop owner's son who's got an idea for some kind of shoe cleaner and Sports Direct have taken it on, the fifteen-year-old is destined for success. The family will be all together on New Year's Eve.

You don't want all those mates to get together again, don't be daft – Tony, Mark, Terry, Malcolm, Susie? No – that's not it. Sat in the back of a pub whilst the teenage guitarist plays? Surely not.

Graham Norton is on at 1035. The new Andy Stewart.

Look over last year's diary. Inconclusive. The year Charlene left London for a better world back in L.A. How glamorous they all said.

Generosity might be the answer. Turn on the radio and hear about how someone decided to do one random generosity act every day for 365 days. Maybe that might help... maybe you won't fail to have somewhere to go on New Year's Eve then.

Fireworks go off outside. The air conditioning hums and keeps the temperature at a precise 25 degrees whilst the homeless shelter against the Tesco. Drunken shouting outside means people are officially having fun and creating memories. Precise temperature or the anarchy of fun? You think back to previous New Years to think when it was right...

And as the midnight minute approaches, you realise that leaving this year will be leaving Mum – stepping just that little bit further away from her memory. You want to be with someone to mask it, shield yourself from it; but instead – maybe it's right – you face it. Watch it go whilst Robbie Williams sings, Jools plays piano and you, hermetically sealed in that hotel room, are somehow going through the necessary experience of losing your Mother, whilst also losing Disco, your youth, your sense of hope.   Embrace it.

You hear the text...

Tony: 'Where you going tonight?'

Me: 'Some club in town.' You lie - wondering why he's belled up – must have had another argument with Anna.

Tony: 'Want to hit the town?'

Tony? Forget all you were thinking - It's like you'd thought it'd be - you can cope without Charlene if you've got your mates - like old times. Do the clubs, New Year's Eve all over again.

Into the Uber and out into the night with renewed purpose, back down London road and into that club with the marquee and the doorman and they wave you in and out comes your cash 'don't worry I'm paying Tony' as you're in again to Cameo and 'Word Up' and there's the silver stilettoes once again and blue sequinned dress and blonde hair flying and the bass bumps into you once again as you escort Tony, your mate, your best mate, into the jungle and you're back – oh yeah – back amongst the palms and step up to the chrome bar before even bothering to look at the twenty five year olds who can only see other twenty five year olds. Orange juice? You sure?

'No wait – do you have any Pernod?'

'Two Pernods?'

A silent nod. Who'd a thought - in 2016?

You let the taste of black liquorice infuse your head. You look around at the last hour and just about everyone is drunk, shouting over your head focused on getting an order in or dancing over on the makeshift dance floor – frantic – oh so frantic to grab this last hour by the balls and somehow not let it escape by creating some form of forced memorable event.

'Here we are then' Tony states the obvious with a certain sarcasm we both know very well whilst using the energy in the room to inspire and observe.

'Who shall we break the heart of tonight?'

'I remember Cameo when it was just 'Single Life'.

'Look at that body - in that dress…'

'We're just a couple of letches.'

'– fifty-five year old letches.'

'I'm fifty-four.'

'Oh well in that case.'

'Anyway – we're not letches if we just stand here – if we score we're players.'

'Yes, but we definitely won't score – so we're letches.' Tony, pessimistic as ever.

'The possibility remains – until that's a definite – we're possible players – anything could happen.'

'Well I'm definitely not asking anyone.'

'Why not?'

'Anna – I've got Anna.'

'So why you out tonight?'

'We both thought...'

'What do you mean - we both thought?'

'You know – you're alone and all – '

'We being you and Anna – taking pity?'

'Not at all.'

'So how long you out for – how long did she let you out for?'

'Couple of hours – midnight – look it's not like that.'

'So, this isn't a real night out at all - I'm the charity case that needs looking after!'

'Look, we're worried about you – we agreed I'd head out and live the nightlife and –

'- really don't bother Tony, there is absolutely no need for charity.'

You both pause and nod as Trussel's 'Love Injection' starts up – a surprise classic in amongst the drudgery of modern nightclub music – but given the DJ it'll change in seconds.

'It's not charity, Kenneth – it's genuine concern.

And you stand and watch and quickly realise Tony's just here for you. Charity. All of a sudden you feel pathetic. Her white dress doesn't fit, the heels are low, men stand about in silly skin-tight jeans trying to look like Tom Hardy. It's a different world, it really was thirty five years ago. Roxy Music – who'd a thought? – 'Loneliness is a crowded room.' Bryan Ferry has the last word it seems. You're off out into the streets and you know where you're going.

Screams of toppling high heels and shouts of loud twenty-five year olds trying to find a mate whilst beered up and pretending not to care, yet desperately trying to find someone on a night like this, before they have to resort to OkayCupid and the stigma of love having not just fell in their lap. Past the taxis, white shirts and pink dresses, past the groups gathered having left it too late, past the doormen wondering whether that twat who threatened to knife him will come back in the next hour, past the dog walker strangely deciding to take it for a walk now – at 1150 – past the two Policemen trying to look vigilant as they chat about past New Year's eves, past the cars trying to get to the event, leaving it too late, telling each other that they've left it too late, through the deserted East Street, past the penniless teenagers hanging out against the rails on the fourth floor of the multi-storey, knocking back the nitrous oxide, down through St Mary's where the families are shut in with the TV on watching Robbie Williams just in case they miss something, as if Armageddon might be due to happen.   And you wonder about this time, what are they expecting to happen?   A clock will strike like it does every day of the year, so maybe this is the one time when we're all, for once, present in the moment - this is the one *real* moment of the year. For once we're not thinking of the next hour, or the past hour, we're thinking of right now; what is our life right now? What has it come to? Who are we with? Have we done well this year? Have we succeeded? Are we surrounded by those we love?   Where *are* the fucking silver palm trees?

So, you keep walking through the council estate just as the first rocket goes off and there you see the white legs of the Itchen Bridge towering above you and arching asymmetrically, but nevertheless beautifully, out over the banks of the river Itchen, where across the half mile stretch of water R.J. Mitchell built the Spitfire before the factory was bombed, but the people of Southampton carried on making them around the city in garages and bus stations. How brilliant was that? Heroes, all…

But now only fireworks shatter the night, sent up from the old city walls as you round the desolate concrete balustrade and start walking the narrow path up the incline and over the arch, just like Joey, Double Jay and Bobby C. in Saturday Night Fever. Walking out of Southampton and up to the apex as you look back at the fireworks now in full swing, single rockets arcing up from isolated towers, as if private dwellers are adding their part to the frenzy of ancipation. Reds, oranges, silver… it seems riotous and yet strangely false as the night moves into morning just like it does every night/day, and everyone has a glass of wine and finds an excuse to be with each other, whether they want it by now or not, they're thinking about where they are right now, and so are you.

As you stand, a car passing dispenses the shouts 'Happy New Year!' And you remember what it was to be seventeen, when drinking was unknown territory, when a mate with a car was special, when you had enough money for one Chinese takeaway a week. You, the kid doing 'A' levels…

But no one is listening to you, and you feel like you felt when Bobby C climbed onto the Verrazano Narrows and tried to do a handstand to impress his friends because no one was listening to *him*. You let them down, you were not there when Tony needed help. That was it, that was the defining moment of your life. And now, just like Bobby C, you needed to do that handstand and prove you had the guts. Anonymity – is the reality. Do that handstand. Prove it...

And you know they'll be watching now – the lone man at midnight on New Year's Eve – now that you've stopped. They'll be squawking their walky-talkies and the bald, middle aged man in his fluorescent yellow will be rising himself from his little cab over at the toll booth and zipping up his jacket, slowly waddling out to the bridge. You've got time enough.

So, here goes, Southampton. New York - London – Paris... as you clamber up unsteadily onto the concrete balustrade, and the Itchen breeze hits you as you try to stay focused by looking at the concrete beneath your feet with the icy wind coming in from Southampton water but you cannot help glancing at the lights and crackling rockets over to your left, the odd piece of drifting smoke from a fusillade of back garden cheap five-pounders – determined to be the last effort – fritters themselves away in short, sharp squeaks and a flash of red; no bomb-blast, no explosion into a mass of orange sparkles, no silver shower of rippling magnesium. Steady now, get your balance, at least 90 feet high here and that water will be like concrete. There it is… the ultimate answer awaits, what man has questioned for centuries… the answer to where do we go… and here you hang in the balance – and death is very close now – and you bend down, rest your hands in front of you and try to set your balance, it's just concrete - like you get on the pavement – no different – except this is 90 feet up and the breeze blows and you wobble as you try to kick your legs up behind you but you never were any good at handstands…

How about a headstand? 50/50 you'll get it right… worth a try, so you take your jacket off and use it as a pillow to rest your head. That's better, set your forehead on the jacket, hands shoulder width apart, now they're watching, now they're stopping, now they're shouting. Too late. You're doing this headstand. And you kick your legs up behind you – not enough – the legs flail and come back to the concrete making you look like you're praying; kick your legs up behind you again and it's there. Hold it. Perfect headstand. And you feel your legs overbalancing and suddenly everything is very real. The New Year, the shouts from the car, the disco – your happiest moments were right there, even in the suffering, the shyness, you just weren't built for asking girls to dance, because you lacked the ability to lose your shame. That's it. Shame.

Lose your shame.

That really is it. If you have no shame then the world opens up. You dance like no one is watching you. You feel closer to New York already, out on the ledge like Phillip Petit, living your life on the high wire at last, walking between the twin towers. It is a moment of great beauty.

And as you balance upside down you remember how you would do the same on the couch at home and claim it helped you think better. Mum carried on knitting, watching Steptoe. In this moment, this all too fleeting moment of clarity, stupidity, near death, things seem beautiful, happy even, for once you're not walking down the same corridor at 0855, you're not marking homework until 6:30, you're not taking your half term holiday in St Ives in February. You're not predictable, you're showing them, you're providing excellent campfire conversation at the barbecues you're not invited to anymore because you're boring. Did you hear what Kenneth did? Remember Kenneth? No, not that one. It's so simple now that you've done it. The legs remain, wavering but your triangle of hands and head is holding you in perfect blance right on the edge of the Itchen Bridge – the well-known suicide location; It's with a sense of regret that you allow the legs to sweep down, down past the balustrade and into the arms of the small group that have now gathered. And they'll have their New Year story too. You've made New Year a real event, all on your own. So simple when you know how.

But you don't let them grab you – you realise just in time and let your legs come forward on to the balustrade, so you stand up, above them, still on stage, still worthy of attention, because the danger is so close. Your legs find the concrete ledge again. Stand up, proud. Disco dancing on the ledge. No one comes near, they just watch, transfixed for once.

'Now, you listen.' You're channelling Bobby C.

Never mind the babble they're all talking – the usual shit – the usual yoga inspired self-help that probably helped get you here. No. With your new-found discovery of loss of shame, you let them see your moves – you can hear it in the distance from the car stereo and Club Classics on Heart FM – The 'Trammps' and 'Disco Inferno' belts out – perfect. And you go into the Travolta move you know so well but don't even dare do in your own living room because who the hell will be embarrassed? Mum isn't here Ken. Life doesn't work like that; you make mistakes and no one really cares, just like you do really beautiful worthy things – and no one really cares either. Mother Theresa? I give you Adolf Hitler – probably lived and experienced just as much happiness and misery as each other. So dance on that balustrade, go for the Russian Cossack thing as Rasputin comes on from the car stereo and you're hopping up and down with your arms folded like an athlete, they stare and marvel and then you remember this is the move you always get wrong...

22: 'Midnight creeps so slowly into hearts of men...'

'Why'd you turn it off?'

'Why don't you come off that ledge?'

'Because you'll all go away if I do.   You'll go on your way, and I'll be just another suicide –

'Now mate...'

'- and we'll be back where we were before.'

'And what's wrong with that?' Says the rotund man disturbed from his warm office where he was watching Robbie bare his chest one more time - live.

'It's a bit lonely that's what.' Funny, Southampton is still looking more exciting than it has done for years.

'I've got a wife and three kids – chimes in the taxi driver - shit – I'm probably lonelier than all of you – kids all got their own TVs, only see them at dinner, mind you maybe that's not such a bad thing.'

'Why do you think I'm volunteering for duty?' Says the newly arrived Policeman.

'To stop people like me.'

'Of course – and it gets me out – better than staying indoors.'

'You too?' You ask, surprised at the sudden self-help meeting.

'Look, never mind about me – ' says the Policeman trying to establish order.

'- new to this?'

'Gimme a chance – not been doing it for long' He edges towards the balustrade to your right – you know what he's up to – but right now you're enjoying the attention. People are taking you seriously and listening - for once. Here's the event you were all looking for.

'Right, well whilst you have a practise....'

'Stop!' He lumbers onto the balustrade and begins to crawl along the balcony like a hippo in a circus on the high-wire – one hand outstretched in some form of symbolic preventative measure – 'you know Kenneth, there are ways of killing yourself without killing yourself.'

Double take. 'You quoting Saturday Night Fever? – and how'd you know my name?'

'I told him.' Tony's voice comes from your left – how'd he get there? Tony is also crawling towards you – on your left – lit up like a scene from a movie by the orange streetlamps lining the bridge. You picture what this must look like from the assorted audience gathering on the road as the traffic begins to hoot its support for this dramatic rescue scene developing – you hear the countdown and realise for you and everyone right here – stuck on their way to something far more important – you have provided them with a New Year to remember... the crowd call out - ten, nine, eight, seven...

Upstaged by a New Year countdown. What the hell is Tony doing out here – did he bring the Police? It's all too late Tony, you go back to your fire in the hearth and Anna and -

The Policeman crawls closer – you know that smug look and note the scar over the left eye. – it's the Disco Nazi.

'A fellow fan of the greatest film ever made?' Personally, I think that was the world at its best.' Disco Nazi had clearly gone and made a career move, but was the same annoying twat you knew many years back.

'You too?' Says Tony, still crawling and finding a common bond whilst you teeter on the edge of a ninety-foot drop.

'Get the hell off the bridge Tony.' Just as he says that a stiff breeze comes in from across Southampton water and blows your heels back against the rail.

'Okay okay - I'm getting down.'

And just as you do your foot catches on that very rail of the balustrade throwing your balance backward, momentarily, but just enough to topple you – the following series f events and thoughts happen in half a second; your arms wave in a desperate attempt to regain the safety of the orange-lit sanctuary that is the bridge and all that life still holds – instant cold sweat – pulse jumps – breathless - sudden realisation that you place too much emphasis on New Year. It's just you needing a family and a sense of 'home' just so you can question it all and probably leave it to 'find' yourself in some South American bar attempting to chat with the Puerto Rican dancer/barmaid – but you'd still be unhappy and on your own but this time with a family you'd left behind and trying to forget whilst they take you to court for maintenance payments. Charlene, Sarah? Icons you couldn't have, so, you stuck them on pedestals and will eternally want what they represent. Unless you attain them, then you'll pigeonhole that away and it'll be something else…

Half a second later.

Slow motion. Bridge, falling away and with this the realisation that your life is ending… right here, right now.

And you hear someone shout 'Happy New Year' but it's amidst gasps because you're toppling – the wrong way… this wasn't the plan - the darkness envelops you and you feel the bite of the ninety-foot breeze grab the back of your neck. You've just discovered dancing, lack of shame, how to live far too late - and it's all disappearing in a glow of orange lamplight…

… and life has become valuable as you see the distant beauty of the assembled revellers and maintenance man disappear into the distance - over the edge for ever…

'Gotcha!' - the Nazi's yellow jacket appears from nowhere like lightning and grabs your right leg - the part of you that is still in touch with the concrete. On your left Tony reaches out – slips as your legs flail for a foot hold – and is suddenly hanging on next to you – but he can't hold on – just by his fast slipping fingertips – you reach across – no – for a moment you both scrabble – reach for his hand - not Tony – but the Nazi's got your legs as he reaches over the side – you've got Tony's arms as he dangles below – you note how the ripples can still be made out, a seagull drifts past underneath – seagulls at midnight? Your right arm muscle screams as he holds on to Tony's wrist and Tony's legs flail and you think of Anna at home and how you're gonna explain this and know that's not going to happen and feel his hand slipping through yours…

As you watch his hand slip out and fall away, you note it stays where it is – it doesn't plunge to the concrete water but somehow stays where it is, then lifts and then his body raises above yours in slow motion… you must be in a dream.

You watch the balding, solitary bridge watchman hoist Tony up and over the side and he is suddenly your rather bashful hero as you hug the man – he has just fished a boathook from somewhere and hauled him up by his belt – with the help of the eighteen-year-old couple who jumped from their car.

Winded. In shock– all air is gone as the Policeman pulls the whole lot of your stupidly winded, useless failure of a body over the side and into the small crowd.

You stand with Tony, breathless, all four of you contemplating the event as if you'd just all come in joint first on the local half marathon, until you realise it's all because of you; you and your inability to cope with Charlene, Mum and being alone. The four of you, three of them recently proven heroes – you bet they can ask women to dance, can dance, can save lives, act in the moment. Heroes. You shake the hand of the embarrassed, corpulent and balding bridge security officer in the day-glo jacket; shake the hand of the Disco Nazi turned Policeman. You need to see Charlene.   One last time.   There's no shame in it. Shame... there's no need for shame at all.

23: '...Burning - you keep my whole body yearning.'

Shivering in a blanket like some marathon runner, you sip a paper cup of sweet machine coffee in hand, rapidly going cold. Ron's the name of the one-time bouncer turned Policeman ('well it's a better pension isn't it?') looks up from his own pathetic cardboard attempt at hot liquid.

'So that was you with the Nile Rogers lookalike?'

'Lookalike?' Surely not – eight years you've been telling that story.

'He was just a local who liked pretending – hah! You fell for that?'

Tony smirks a 'told you so.'

'Anyway - we used to call you the Disco Nazi.'

'I seem to remember you never danced.'

'Well I also wasn't over eighteen either - in an over 25s club – you let us through – how about that?'

'I knew that.'

'How – how could you know that?'

'Easy - let them in all the time.'

'You could tell I wasn't over eighteen?'

'Yep.'

'So, why'd you let us in?'

'In your case? Pity.'

'Pity?'

'Yeah – thought I'd give you a break – out of the kindness of my heart.'

'Well, *I* danced.' Says Tony.

'Who needs enemies when you have friends?' You think to yourself – then remember what happened tonight.

You sip the luke-warm liquid and wonder how Mum would feel about all this. You craving attention, almost wiping out your best mate. Memorable for all the wrong reasons.

'...So, I thought – might as well join the Police – help the community rather than kick them out of clubs – better money too – lonely job though. Don't make any friends apart from other bouncers really - but disco? Best time ever – never been the same since oh – 1981? Suddenly the clothing got cheaper, twelve inch singles stopped, Top Rank closed, I kept on with the bouncer work but it wasn't the same. We all need people – at the end of the day no man is an island, that's Shakespeare.'

'John Donne –'

'Definitely Shakespeare.'

'Whatever – thanks anyway for – y'know.' He actually did save your life.

'Anyone would do the same, wouldn't they? Just happened to be me.'

Heroes – you've come across them before, they always dismiss your attempts to admire their courage, their quick thinking, their instinctive, decisive action. It's a mystical power you just don't seem to have – and all in this walking cliché of an ex-bouncer.

'So where's she now?'

'Who?'

'The woman – it's always a woman.'

'What – you mean – why I was up there - ?'

'Yeah – where's she now – should we call her?'

'It's not about a woman.'

'Yeah it is – and she's in L.A.' Pipes in Tony – thanks a lot.

'L.A.? As in Los Angeles?'

'We broke up last year.'

'It's always over some woman.' He sips his luke-warm soup and sums it up with that turn of the head you hate from all those years ago – as if he has the monopoly on great truths. You ponder the injustice that allows twats to save lives.

'Bit more to it than that.'

'Can't live with 'em, can't leave 'em on the pavement.'

Get me out of here you think to yourself – then a text from Charlene arrives with a ping.

Charlene - 'Clubbing?'

'Nope.'

'No? So what did you do?'

'Nothing - no big deal.'

'Must have done something.'

'I learnt to dance.'

'That's a massive big deal.'

'Not anymore.'

'How?'

'How is it not a massive big deal?'

'No – how did you learn to dance?'

'By forgetting about you.'

'Don't blame you. The moment you achieve something you don't care anymore.'

'You mean the dancing?'

'Yeah – so you can dance – massive step for you – believe me I know how big that is for you – now you don't care – like it never mattered – like you've forgotten what it meant to you already.'

You ponder what the hell she means.

'I just realise how trivial it all was.'

'It didn't used to be.'

'So – why'd she leave?' Asks Ron.

'I guess living in a flat is different to hanging out in a disco.'

'With Disco no-one ever takes you seriously.' His massive bulk rustles under the yellow Police stab jacket. He stares into the bottom of his cup, lost, temporarily in limbo, then he rubs his eyes in seeming bewilderment before checking his phone.

'I always was against mobile phones – just reminding you how few friends you have – and the few you have don't want to talk to you.'   He puts the phone back in his heavy-duty waterproof pouch and busies himself with locating his walky-talky on his shoulder, stowing his notebook in his breast pocket and then focuses on his torch. On – off – yep – works. All the time you're watching.

'Well now – are you both gonna be okay?   You nod your assurances and realise you'd better be going, but you've begun to see Ron in a different light all of a sudden and ask a question you already know the answer to:

'You not find it hard – what with family and that – having to be on duty?'

'Not really – there is no family.'

'No wife?'

'Nope. Nearly – but couldn't really be bothered with all that.'

'Really – couldn't be bothered?'

'Well, she couldn't be bothered, I definitely wanted kids but - well – long time ago.'

'Too much trouble anyway.' You throw in by way of support. 'Only Tony here got himself sorted.' Tony smiles apologetically.

Ron takes a breath, sips his cold coffee and shifts his bulky yellow nylon jerkin and even bulkier utility belt around his mid-drift and you realise he needs to get out there and dodge some more knives, bottles and perhaps save another suicidal idiot and his mate from certain oblivion – by way of distraction.

'Truth is – 'Ron inspects the inside of his Policeman's helmet. 'I never really met the right woman.   Lasted seven years – but – it just didn't work out – next thing you're fifty. Still – who needs 'em - eh?'

'You should come with us.'

'Us?' Says Tony.

'Yeah 'us', we've got to be where it's 'at'. Southampton is not the place, I've decided.'

'It used to be – it's always somewhere else with you.'

'Maybe we've just outgrown it – you, me – Ron even.'

'So where is *the* place all of sudden?' Enquires Ron, pausing at the door.

'Where dreams come true.'

'I'm not going to Oceana if that's what you're suggesting.' He puts his helmet on.

'No Ron, you've got to think bigger – Tony – you've got to break away from your workaday life, Ron – Tony, Ron - you all need this as much as me.'

'Where the hell are you suggesting? Not London – nope – forget it.'

'I've got to be getting back' Tony checks his watch.

24: 'Leavin' on the midnight plane...'

This time the sea of orange and white lights spread up the hillside and continue over the horizon and into the early morning mist. L.A is no longer a dream – it spreads out beneath you – momentarily vulnerable as you fly high above and look down upon these mere mortals who will soon become real, live Americans in the city of opportunity. Even from the sky it's too big – the street lights head off into the distance, over the hill on the horizon and keep on going. Portsmouth doesn't have early morning mist, just sleet and the occasional drizzle.

Moby Dick has taken you about seven years so far – and you're on the last page, Tony is just finishing the Westworld TV series whilst Ron plays the retro in-flight racing game - which has provided endless merriment for him all the way from Heathrow. In the last ten minutes he's moved onto the photos on his mobile phone.

'Here - have a look at this.'

Ron taps his phone and spins it round for you both to see. Tony pulls out his earphones, you re-adjust yourself from descending to the bottom of the ocean with the Peaquod.

'Top Rank! - about 1980.'

You pass the phone around and note the blurred quality, but you can still make out the permed hair, the Hawaiian shirts, the seventeen-year-old builds, the groups of males, the groups of girls, the glitz, the community. And there's Odyssey, bottom right, you know because you were there...

You zoom in one the photo to someone on someone else's shoulders.

'See that guy?'

'Yeah?'

'That's Tony – and the head between the legs – me.'

'What's the chances of that?'

'Here gimme that – you're right – Odyssey.'   We survey the blurred image like the Mona Lisa has just appeared on the antiques roadshow.

'You know it was Tony who got Odyssey in?'

'I got them in.' Says Ron all indignant.

'Hang on – who said we should choose Odyssey?'

'I asked some punters what they would – bloody hell –'

'That was us!'

And for a moment all three of you feel you are responsible for the official arrival of Disco in Southampton as the engine note changes and flaps slowly extend on the wing next to the window as the American accent sounds more confident over home territory:

Ladies and Gentlemen, we are now approaching Los Angeles International Airport, where the early morning.

'What's up Tony?'

'Nothing - I'm just worried about Anna - that's all.'

'Still?' Ron, diplomatic as ever.

'I haven't been home and she still thinks I'm in Southampton.'

Ron reacts with the compassion of a robot 'Looks like I'm the only one who's going to have any fun - listen in; we're here now and our mission is to make sure Kenneth meets his lady and wins her back. Anything else is a bonus… comprendi?'

'No one says 'comprendi' anymore - 'cept in Mafia films.'

Ron goes back to his video games – he has the option of 'Ninja' by Eric Van Lustbader but chooses instead the car race along with getting his elbow knocked by passers-by in the aisle seat (fast access in case of hijack).

Tony – on the other side in the window seat is transfixed by the sea of lights below and the sense of guiltily enjoying being in the wrong place.

'So... Tony decides the time is right to throw down the earphones and confront the question as the gears clunks down.

'...what the hell were you thinking?' You both know what he's referring to.

'Don't really know.' Is your honest answer.

'Yes you do, you wanted to kill yourself – What the hell – I mean – shit – don't you want to talk about it at least?'

'Yeah – maybe – if you're listening.'

'So - what *were* you thinking?'

'I just – it's just that I want friends – friends I can talk through the night with – sometimes.'

'Well – you can.'

'Yeah but – it's not really true – is it? Imagine if I belled you up at like 2am – hey Tony – let's meet up and have a chat – because I'm having a hard time. Not gonna happen is it?'

Tony has no answer. Looks out at the black coming up to meet us.

'I just want someone to be on the same page as me – to hang out – no – not on the same page – more like you – married, set up, and yet still wanting to spend the odd evening with me. And not because Anna told you to out of pity.'

'I've just got so much on.'

'Course you have. Quite right too, if you had nothing on you wouldn't be a married guy with a house and children and a life. It's just that I want that vindication – that sense of still being -` you gesture like some scientist explaining cold fusion – 'still being part of the journey. I feel like I'm not part of anyone's journey anymore – there's no joint effort that takes us into the small hours of discos and late-night burgers and shared experience of Stevie Wonder in a car with mates and women and loud music that still buzzes when you get home and you're still dazed the next morning.'

'And that makes you want to kill yourself?'

'No.'

'Right, then what?'

'Just got a little bit carried away.'

'A little bit carried away?'

'Yeah – sorry about that.' You smile sheepishly.

'So, what's to stop you doing it again?'

'Up on that bridge Tony, I discovered something – whilst doing that handstand – nearly toppling over – a moment of clarity.'

'Is that before you let me go or after?'

'Just before – sorry - It was a moment of discovery - I felt my legs going over – then swung back, got up, felt free, danced. Didn't care. Dunno what it was, lost my shame. Now that's a discovery. I now know – I can dance. And other stuff. *Then* I fell off.'

'So that's it? Loss of shame is your great discovery?'

'That is it. Shame. Think what it stops us from doing.'

'Stops us from behaving like bloody idiots.'

'True, but also stops us from doing things that'd make our parents disappointed in us – like giving up that job that you hate.'

'Sleeping with prostitutes.'

'Going to lap dancing bars.'

'Dancing badly.'

'I'm over it.'

Ron: 'Look at that view – you know we spend our lives looking forward to things - trying to get to that place – that event – that sense of where it's at – and here we are officially arriving at the home of 'where it's at' and I guarantee we'll find people saying 'this ain't where it's at – you need to go there – where the grass is greener – like Palm Springs or Rodeo Drive or - Santa Monica beach!

'Ha - maybe.'

'I think at Santa Monica beach they'll be a guy going 'wish I could be in cool, drizzly Portsmouth or sunny Southsea common right now.'

'You think?'

Tony sighs – he knows he wanted to come and for once just went on instinct – and that's why you know him – despite all his responsibility and sense of duty – he can suddenly throw it all in the air and get on a plane.

'Look, Ken, can I speak – frankly?'

You nod, head down, ready to accept the harsh but honest observation coming your way:

'You never feel like you're in the moment – so even though I think you're often in the centre of amazing things – you never accept that you are – like in the disco days you felt there was a world out there you had to discover – so you went after it and joined the Army. Then you felt there was a world out there outside and so you chased after it – and came back here by your own design you're definitely not in the moment, always wanting to be where there's a mystical party going on - so you don't appreciate that where you are is ever the right time. Imagine if you did? Imagine if you decided that where you were was the best it could be? The best life you could possibly be living? Imagine that!'

'What – like even in a classroom with a bunch of pissed-off students on a Monday morning you're telling me I need to consider myself in the best possible scenario?'

'Yep – that you chose that path and even if Monday morning is a bag of shit – in the long run it's all part of your plan – which it is – isn't it?' Imagine if you thought like that – not saying I'm right – just saying – if you did – that where you are is 'where it's at' – and you know what?   That would be where it *is* at. Maybe.'

'The readiness is all...'

'Sorry lads – just overhearing your philosophical discussion – surely this is why we're all on this trip – if we can't accept *this* city is where it's at then we better start looking at other planets.'

'Thank's Ron.'

'Just saying.'

Clunk – the Dreamliner touches down and you're there – ready to find where it's at.

'Well here we are gents. Los Angeles International.' Ron announces. 'I will proceed to locate a reasonable priced mode of transport and I recommend you both recce baggage carousel nine.'

'How do you know its nine?'

'Prior planning Kenneth, I checked with Virgin SOP.'

'SOP'? Asks Tony sheepishly.

'Standard Operating Procedure' answers Ron proudly. You yawn.

Wait in queues half asleep, shuffle in line, stamp, fingerprint, shoes off, shoes on. Check your belt sir... welcome - next...

And you walk out into the dry, warm air doing up your shoes and putting your belt back on and are already noticing how everything seems – bigger – brighter –

parched by the stronger sunlight – they need more efficient air conditioning, the signs need to be more brutal – No parking – armed guards – danger of death – do not cross the line sir. You can feel that album cover already – yes – this is the land of the Kool and the Gang album cover.

Out onto the pull in area, men in peaked caps, baggage in tow, no stopping, somehow your phone works and the Uber app finds you a ride.

'27th Avenue, 1980 Ocean Front Walk please.'

You sit quietly whilst the Uber Prius whispers you through the early morning wide open streets and the glimpse of early dawn feels like a rebirth, a new start, an escape. Ron and Tony doze whilst you take in everything in a daze. Al Jarreau sings 'Morning mister shoe shine man...'

You drift past posters of the local spa gymnasium holistic health centre, past the organic noodle shop, past cool Mexican restaurants, past Mexican women lining up their stalls with the usual tamales, trinkets and cell-phone gadgets. Past the wooden Italian mansions with neatly cut palms touched by the first golden glint of dawn at their tips, past the scattered palm debris, the wires and wood, past the sun-bleached poster blue-boarded houses.

'Millionaires paradise? Looks like it's all about to fall down with the first gust of wind.' Ron's woken up.

'Earthquake.' Says the Uber driver.

'What's that?' Ron isn't too sure how to react to such information.

'They build them out of wood in case of earthquake – means you don't get whole load of bricks on your head man.' The Uber driver's name is a Mexican named Antonio.

'Right – good idea – but they still look rather simple – cheap even.'

'That's cos they spent all their money getting here' croaks Tony.

And finally, into the curious mix of sea air, telephone wires, wood and concrete housing intercut with overgrown palm bordered alleyways belying a rental value in the millions because they all back directly on to the beach that is - Venice, the sign swinging like a forgotten tourist resort in the half-light that is 5am. And yet the Uber's window is open, the air is warm. How strange. Hayling Island it isn't.

Finally, abruptly and rudely; a large, white, concrete and glass geometric zig zag juts out over the beach and taunts you with its extravagance. You pull up and note that a piece of sculpted driftwood stands sentinel on the balcony amidst two white chairs and three giant halogen lights lay embedded in the concrete whiteness above ready to spotlight you below as unworthy of even wandering into the vicinity of this design wonder-piece. You walk around the surrounding painted grey wall and arrive at the gate, flanked by palm bushes. The number is etched expensively into a sun-bleached and sand-blasted piece of slate set in a concrete bollard: 1980: Of course. Where else would she end up? A door is set into the stucco white wall and lies flush, almost invisible, whilst tinted glass juts out and glints reflectively from the foliage and unkempt palms, like a spaceship amongst the jungle. You're not sure where it ends, or starts.

Ron and Tony shake your hand, wish you luck, wave your protests away with the strangely moving gesture of wanting to help someone out and tell you they'll be in touch for the evening. The Prius silently slips off into the distance like a scene from Space 1999 in early morning Santa Monica. Has music taken you this far?

You walk up the path, press the buzzer and wait. You think back to summer holidays when you called on friends who were always away – on holiday – you stood at their front doors, knocking nervously until they got back so you could recommence games of cricket or three and in with a football, but that sense of being somewhere at the wrong time or the wrong place – or both - never left you. Misfit – definitely NOT where it's at. Their parents couldn't fathom you out and asked why you always seemed to be that boy hanging about with no-one to play with.

A white robe skims the shining marble, the door silently opens and you're back in the moment – she wipes away the sleep from her dark brown eyes. She hugs you with a real hug like dancers give that threaten your ribs, kisses your cheek and you smell - ? 1980 - like it never left.

'Can't believe you're here.'

So far so good, you sit and hold each other in the very window you were moments ago looking up at and wonder what this all means. Dozing, sleeping on some luxurious white leather party sofa that glimpses the palm-lined beach in front. Finally. But you know it can't last as you drift off.

You're awoken by the sound of a fridge opening in the distance – the open plan dining room come lounge is corrupted by the corpulent figure of a man in a dressing gown opening soya milk and getting ready to cook. Grey hair, successful, previous marriage, distinguished.

'Sorry to wake you – you want any breakfast?'

'No – er no thank you – who are you?'

'Oh, sorry – I'm Ryan - I live here.' He marches over and goes to shake your hand like a military operation. You have no choice.

'With Charlene?'

'Yes.'

'Oh - right.'

'Can I get you anything?'

'No – no – oh what the hell – got any – what do they eat for breakfast in California?'

'Cale, Quinoa with some Muesli?'

'Really?'

'Some probably do – not me – I prefer croissants.'

'That's fine by me.'

The beach slowly comes to life below the overhang – detached and yet amongst it– you stare down at the quiet, placid highway of skateboards, joggers, runners, cyclists and roller-bladers shining bright in the early light. Slowly you begin to quietly, internally laugh at the thought she could ever be anything but a dream.

'That's certainly a view' which is like saying a Rolls Royce is a car. You expect the usual reaction – 'yeah but the rent is outrageous' or 'it's okay but we're moving to an even better place soon' – the usual. But instead you get...

'Yep. This is it.' He stands staring, unwary, unpretentious, taking it all in as if he's just discovered it. He's wider than you, short beard, watching the skateboarder drift past below as he turns his attention to you and hands you the fresh pastry.

'Soya okay?'

Must be the milk - so you nod. The light, the sprung wooden floor, the rubber plants and the open plan brutalist vastness remind you of all your album covers and Athena posters come together at the same time. More Kraftwerk than Chic. You feel you should be wearing a red shirt and a black leather tie.

He turns to you 'So let me get this straight - you've really just come – on impulse - all the way from the UK – from Southampton?'

You take a deep breath of embarrassment.

'Oh I'm sorry – Max this is Kenneth – Kenneth this is Max.' Charlene floats in wearing a white silk trouser suit and criss- crosses her arms by way of an introduction like a vogueing dancer, her eyes still half open.

'What do you do?'

'Capitol.'

'What's that?'

'Oh sorry – Capitol Records – big record company in the city.'

'He knows who Capitol Records are, Max.'

'Okay but he did ask.'

'Yes I did Charlene – thanks though – that's big – is that like - production?'

Yeah – kinda.'

You note the grand piano in a distant corner. Skills, abilities and income you cannot even fathom wander past your feeble sense of understanding right now. You feel elevated to their lifestyle, momentarily, before remembering you have nothing to do with this. Pathetic. To think you could attain a woman with tastes like this for even a moment. You smell fresh leather like the inside of a new car and wonder how, of all the women you didn't ask, you actually ask the one who has most reason to refuse you.

Disco, the great leveller.

'Well, you must have a lot to talk about – good to meet you.'   He drops his plate on the side of a stainless-steel sink that nestles in the concrete wall with a built-in tap, which immediately turns on for ten seconds before self-cancelling. He disappears down a distant white corridor. There appear to be no doors, just alcoves that lead somewhere down dark, cool, concrete walls interspersed with full length glass panels that glimpse the outside through a brown tint.

'I can't believe – is this where you live?

'It is where we live.'

'His money?'

She pauses and even with her half-awake eyes she cuts you a look that you know and love:

'Sorry? Who the hell are you again?'

'Just asking.'

'Few ground rules Kenneth – if you don't mind – don't assume.'

'Alright alright – I'm sorry – I'm tired – I'm shocked at this place. That's all.'

'Yeah well… remember that advert I was auditioning for?'

'You were always auditioning.'

'The make-up one - well anyway - I got it.'

'Oh – good on you.'

'For L'Oreal.'

'Who – okay that's big.'

'Yeah well – went nationwide.'

'That must be enough for a down-payment.'

'No, we went halves.'

'You did what - shit.'

'Not bad for a two-bit has-been dancer huh?'

'I didn't say anything.'

'No but you were thinking it.'

'Hey – I'm pleased you fell on your feet okay – I really am.'

'Really? – After me leaving you in London?'

'Let me get back to you on that.'

'Wanna learn to Surf?'

'What - now?'

'Right now.'

'Lifetime ambition just to stand up – you know that.'

'Let's go then.'

So you follow her out – she's still in her silk trouser suit which somehow becomes a bikini as you run out onto the half mile of sand between you and the pacific, both of you barefoot, boards in hand and she dives in ahead of you like a practised surfer chick who's lived on the beach all her life, you wade out cautiously and get knocked by every wave that strikes the board head on.

'Hey - like this.'

And all you see is a brief paddle, two brown legs and her sculpted profile that sails past you like some advert for Blue Stratos as she rides the wave and disappears towards the shore. Followed by half an hour of you falling off.

She gathers her white silk and throws it over her drying, sandy bikini and disappears inside. You walk back, let yourself in like her long-time companion who lives there, hoping the passing skateboarders see you for some successful LA producer as you take your time opening the gate. She's at the window, drinking some green mixture.

'Have some – Celery, Cucumber, Guava.'

And now you're jogging, up to Santa Monica and back down to Venice before you find yourself in the

January sun eating noodles and thinking about the future.

'Is he for keeps then?'

'I don't know – never mind that - what's this about you being able to dance?'

Distant banging on the door downstairs and you know no one bangs like that in Venice Beach.

'Who the hell?'

Ron and Tony stand before Charlene; Tony already decked out like an album cover with Ray Bans and Hawaiian shirt, Ron in a parka.

'He left all his clothes in the cab.'

Ron stands at attention as if expecting a bollocking.'

'Charlene this is – Tony you know and – Ron – man who saved my life on the bridge.'

'You're the guy?'

'Just doing my job.'

Ron adopts a casual smile, leans on a table and sends a thin, small and stupidly expensive glass vase to its doom. Charlene says 'it's nothing' and clears up whilst Ron tries to help by picking up tiny pieces of glass, realises he can't and returns to standing stock still in fear of knocking something else over.

'Nice view' says Ron in classic understatement.

'Thank you - so... how long you all here for?'

'Two days.'

'Two days?'

'Two days.'

'That's madness - that means you've got one night...

'You said it.'

'Then we gotta go out tonight.'

'Any recommendations?'

'We're going to Mojito's.

'Mojito's?'

'It's a club.'

You're in amongst the crowd of girls in bad ripped jeans and crop tops and the guys are in braces and high waisted trousers - and there's you in a suit – dancing at The Mojito in downtown LA, some converted cinema made into a super slick nightclub where the doorman nods at Charlene and all four of you wander in ahead of the queuing crowd – Ron still with his parka on is initially refused but luckily a word from Charlene and he immediately adopts the arrogance of a VIP as he's waived through - and then you with your leftover New Year's Eve suit – you feel like the shabby, reclusive millionaire as Cheryl Lynn's classic 'Got to be Real' is cutting up the floor, but the feet don't quite move the way you want to, you feel stiff, like always…

'Bend your knees Ken'

'I am'

'Relax.'

Nightmare. You're back there again.

'Hey don't worry – it's cool.'

You retreat to the sanctity of the bar. Defeated. It's the little things – right now...'there are ways of killing yourself without killing yourself...' the voice comes from nowhere... Ron, leaning over with that scarred face and friendly, self-satisfied grin. Parka furry hood. Bastard, but he's right.

Remember – shame. So you catch the eye of the woman in a waistcoat behind the bar and she pours you a whisky and you sip once before putting it down purposefully and walking straight out amongst those younger bodies that you don't really care about anymore and let Cheryl Lynn take you away as you think back twenty-four hours to last night on the bridge, and how you nearly lost Tony, how you lost that shame just for that moment and realise you have no job to go back to, that it's Uber driving from here on – if you can afford a car. You're free-falling. Free. You forgot yourself for a moment and Sylvester kicks in – green and blue glitter surround you. No one is here. Mum isn't there to be embarrassed for you, Charlene is with someone else, the whole trip is pretty-well pointless - If you let it be... So no one is watching and nothing matters. So why not dance? The music is good, the bass is here, Sylvester's your friend. You're dancing... out here in Los Angeles. The glitter is around, the disco ball spins and casts those shadows just like 1979 all over again, you've made it, survived.

'Ron's pulled' shouts Tony from the floor.

No he hasn't – he's somehow momentarily addressing some exotic beauty at the bar. You await the slapped face or the turned-up nose. For some reason Ron waves you over.

'Let me introduce my good friends Tony and Kenneth – this is Juanita.'

'Hey Kenneth – Tony - what up man?' Her smile explodes from her face and just about eclipses her leopard-clad bosom as the Pina Colada's are exchanged to shake hands. You don't know where to look.

'Hey Juanita!' Shouts Charlene and suddenly you're amongst dancers as a voice sounds from the stage:

'And now, all the way from Havana, Cuba, Juanita Mendoza!'

And the woman you were talking to? That smile? Hits the floor and performs the most exact series of moves all with that beaming smile before you realise she's performing - Is attacking the audience right now to the tune of 'Come on Baby light my Fire' – and you slowly realise that she's the dancer in a downtown LA club. That's officially cool beyond Granny's, beyond the Top Rank, beyond Nero's.

'Old friend' says Charlene, handing you and Tony a Whiskey. 'And looks like Ron's got a *new* friend.'

'Says she likes Policemen.' Announces Ron, bewildered.

'In that Parka?'

'Even in this parka - but if she's Cuban - isn't she a Communist?'

'Oh I guess that'll put a stop to it then.'

Charlene watches Ron's face, in fact you all do. Ron ponders his life for a moment, sips his Pina Colada with little umbrella, looks around at the club.

'What do you think I am – some kind of idiot?'

The Uber dispenses Ron and Juanita back at her place in Echo Park, drops Tony at the Motel, whilst Charlene comes into your room with the lights on a chain and the dusty blinds.

'So what happens now? When do you have to go back to work?'

'I'm not going back.'

'What you going to do?'

'I don't know – I was kinda hoping you were single – silly me.'

'You thought I was single?'

'You never said.'

'So you came out here – just to see me?'

'Yep.'

'Oh no! You came out here to try one last chance.'

'I know – stupid.'

' – how romantic.'

'Yeah – I know – and stupid.'

'Not stupid.' Silence. She pulls up the blinds and perches on the window-sill, looks out the window at downtown LA and the Burger King sign on the corner, ponders their complete lack of romance. The wires are exposed on the empty motel sign that has long been dismantled, or fallen off. Despite the ants and the chained-up lights, you have a view.

'You want to be friends?' It feels like a punch, but you know it's meant like a kiss.

'I'd like to be friends with you.'

'Do you think you know how? Do you think you could be friends with a girl? Could you stand that?' She smiles at you – already a beautiful friend.

'The truth? I don't know… I could try. That's all I can say.'

'OK Tony Manero, let's be friends, all right? We'll just be friends.

'All right.' And she reaches out her hand to you across the view of a parking lot.

'Friends, man.' And you hold your hand in hers.

Ping. The Uber is here.

'I'll still be in contact – random-like – to pester you.'

Some us want to place our love in a box and own it. But it won't always be owned, or lived with, or compromised. You can know it, have fun with it, but if you want more with her, then find someone else. Charlene – it might be that all your dreams of girl on the album cover led you to nothing more than loneliness – but one thing you do have is the Nightlife, on the end of a phone – just when you don't expect it. Yeah, maybe you'll let her pester you after all.

Maybe the seventeen-year-old dancer in the ski jersey in the clubs in '79 met the right woman, had the kids, the whole package. Maybe all those Pompey girls in the silver high heels are sat around watching daytime TV now, maybe they're treating those days as rather tacky, quaint. Maybe they lived the life we all thought we wanted to live – and had a wild New Year's Eve party around the fireside this year. But they made no discovery like you did tonight, and somehow it doesn't feel right to head back to your life in London.

So, as you bed down for the night under the stars in your cheap motel, under the ant-ridden sheets, the Burger King sign outside standing sentinel, you feel - mighty real in fact. It's no longer out there, hidden away under those palm trees; you did it - you became your own personal album cover. You are where it's at – at last. Denied, refused, but attempted, without shame.

25: Work, again.

The photocopier's not working (needs toner and there's no paper)

Formal Assessments are due in next week.

The History teacher is off sick and his lesson needs to be covered.

The usual eight students who can be bothered to turn up stand patiently, half asleep, outside the classroom in the flickering neon light, with peeling posters and an abandoned water dispenser surrounding them.

'Kenneth, I'm afraid we have to set a disciplinary due to your behaviour with respect of your threatening to punch a student due to his repeated use of a mobile phone whilst in your lesson.'

You wait patiently for him to finish. Nod, agree, tell them you can save them a lot of bother.

'I beg your pardon?'

'I'm resigning, as of today.'

Silence. No big deal. Probably for the best.

'Could we talk about this a moment please, Kenneth?'

Turns out it would jeopardise a lot of students' results. Especially those who don't turn up to lessons.

'Maybe we can talk about the disciplinary?'

26: Parallel lines, parallel life

'Every year it's the same, why don't we do something a bit different?'

She steers the second hand Corsa into Sainsburys and gives you that look:

'Because we haven't got the money and we promised we'd be spending New Year with them, besides there's your Dad to keep an eye on.'

Sam, having just hit eighteen, lounges on the sofa and texts on the phone. You only had the one kid, you figured that was all you could afford on your wage at the dole office. Since then you put your wages together, put down the deposit on a semi' in the late eighties and got on the property ladder just before the boom slumped and negative equity kicked in, but it didn't matter because you kept the place on the outskirts of Southampton and near the sea.

You eventually ditched the dole office job and ended up driving the bus round Fareham, past all the old haunts of your teenage years. Maybe you didn't achieve all you set out to do all those years ago; you remember with a smile, once wanting to join the Army. Imagine that? – the mere thought sends a chill down one side of you. One week away with the

Territorials and you were homesick for the disco and your mates.

You don't regret it for a minute.   Okay, maybe you'd have a glamorous wife and a fast car, flying an airliner round the world and living in a stately mansion near Heathrow airport – maybe you'd be able to afford more children and suggest they do University rather than go to work at the nearest B+Q, but what of it – you didn't need it. They don't either. You've got Sky plus, a library of box sets, Netflix and the latest in surround sound. What more could you need? Seriously.

'For old acquaintance be forgot and never brought to mind…' and so you link arms across the carpet with Malcolm and Susie, Tony and Anna, the cat and the gerbils, all happily gathered for your umpteenth New Year's Eve together, welcoming it in, some music, discussion on the latest change from digital to vinyl, whilst the girls talk about hairdressing and you wonder where the time went, how little Robert's going to start work soon, then you and Helen can go on a cruise. Maybe move nearer to Southampton. Maybe join that fitness gym – new year's resolution, less chocolate, lose weight, get fit. Remember those days with the Territorials? Remember how fit you were? What happened? Marriage, kids, that's what happened.

Well, enough of the family get together – you've had a few but hell – take a chance – time to drive the lot home.

You all wearily pile into the Corsa and drive out from Shirley and out on to the main road, passing through the late-night stragglers who forgot to plan their get home strategy. One figure walks alone towards the bridge.

'That geezer looks like you'.

'Does a bit.'

'Ah well, back to the old grindstone…'

27: Club Tropicana

'Where are you?'

'Looks to me like a beach.'

'What beach? You know you've got triple English A2 this morning.'

'You know I'm on a beach.'

'Right, well, what the hell are you thinking?'

'Take the class - you can be the hero.'

'You know you're letting the whole class down.'

'For fifteen years I've not let them down... I'll live with the shame.'

28: Spirits Having Flown

'Aren't you my teacher?'

'Was.'

'Oh right – what you doing in here?'

'I'm your driver.'

'You?'

'Yes, me.'

'Hah! Hey wicked – guess what – this geezer was my teacher last year.'

'Hehe – right mate – what happened – got in trouble?'

'Not really.'

'So we can say what we like to you now then?'

'Not really.'

'Yeah we can – you're our driver now.'

'No I'm not – off you go.'

'What you on about?'

'I couldn't choose who I taught, but I can choose what twats I drive.   Bye.'

Barry Gibb echoes out of the speakers.

Yes, maybe you'll take a night off.

This is Tony Manero's Hardware store.

This isn't killing yourself.

This is where it's at.

Phone buzzes next to you.

'Hi Kenneth.'

'Hello? Who is it?'

'Sarah.'

'Sarah - Craig?   Haven't heard from you in years!'

'Not since you dumped me in Billionaires.'

'I didn't dump you – you weren't interested.'

'True.'

'So - what do I owe the pleasure to?

'Just checking how you are – how are you?'

'Fine – I'm doing just great actually - so you don't want another date?'

'Nope – he leaves me alone – I leave him alone – we're good.'

'So – just a social call?'

'I guess.'

'I can do that.'

'Good –'

And you ponder the dreaded friendzone and wonder if it's really that bad... what were you after? Whatever it was, conversation with a beautiful woman isn't so bad, right now, in your white limo...

The End

Printed in Great Britain
by Amazon